WHEEL MAN

WHEEL MAN

MARCIA CALHOUN FORECKI

LIBRARY TALES PUBLISHING

Published by Glass Compass Press, LLC
under the Library Tales Publishing imprint.

Library Tales Publishing is a trademark of
Morgan Entertainment Group, LLC, used under license.

Distributed by Empire City Press, LLC
www.librarytalespublishing.com
www.empirecitypress.com
www.glasscompasspress.com

ISBN
9798894410302
9798894410821

First Edition, 2026
Printed in the United States of America

PREFACE

In the hardwood forest on the Missouri side of the Mississippi River, red fox kits are born in April. In the woods near Cinque Hommes Creek, cool spring rain drizzles on the young leaves of shagbark hickory, black walnut, and red cedar trees, and drops in a mist onto the undergrowth. Beneath the sodden leaves, snug in a den lined with his mother's fur, a blind red fox kit sniffs the rich earth above. When the kit's eyes open and his growing den mates begin to scuffle for their share of space, the instinct to run will stir him.

I

GORDY

Saturday was my fifteenth birthday. By Monday, 10:00 am at the latest, I would walk out of the driver's license office with a Missouri Learner's Permit: "*Gordon McCann is hereby permitted to drive in the State of Missouri (with a licensed driver).*" What sweet, sweet words. Next, all I'd need was a babe to put my arm around as I cruised down life's highway. The family birthday barbecue was planned for Saturday afternoon.

Pop and I were split on whether I should receive my "big" birthday present before or after the party. For safety's sake, Pop insisted on making the presentation after. "There will be two children at the party, and rather rambunctious ones at that."

I woke up early on Friday, April 22, 1955, the day before my birthday for those taking notes. Usually, I was the last person in the house to rise. I was never in a hurry to leave my bed. The solitary bathroom in the house was certain to be occupied. The ratio of persons to potty-room was 4.5:1. The person-and-a-half in the family was my little sister Julie. She fiddled around in there like the Queen of Sheba, so Pop said. She was ten years old, always tried to act older, and was as annoying as a toddler.

That morning was no exception. Julie sang a full medley in front of the bathroom mirror while brushing her hair. If Mom or Pop rapped on the door and asked her to snap it up, Julie would sing a formal "Amen," like she was in church, and flush the toilet. Subtle. I asked her through the door to please give a guy a break. She said, "Go outside if you can't hold it. Boys are built to pee outside anyway."

Saturday morning, my first full day as a fifteen-year-old, began with a shake. "Rise and shine, Mister."

"What's up?" I croaked, lifting myself onto one elbow. I glanced out my bedroom window. The sun was still considering whether it would rise today.

"I want to get those spruce saplings your mother has been asking for all winter," Pop said.

Saplings? Who was I, Johnny Appleseed? "Can't we wait until later?"

"Do you know how slowly trees grow?" scoffed Pop. He walked quietly down the creaking stairs to the kitchen. I pulled on pants and a shirt over my pajamas and joined him.

"Let's go," I said, slapping Pop on the back as he filled his Thermos with coffee. Pop pretended my slap was strong enough to push him forward. He pretended to stumble. Sometimes he acted as goofy as "Uncle" Phil. They served in the Army together. They were best friends, practically brothers, but so different. Pop was the always clean, always shaved, tucked-in-shirt Sergeant. His flat top haircut seemed never to grow a lick. Pop was consistent in his appearance and in how he treated people—with respect, or at least they were given the benefit of the doubt.

Private Phil Toomey was the opposite in every way. My family saw him as a good-natured and hard-working guy. He lived alone on his parents' small farm, which fed him and not much more. Uncle Phil was devoted to Pop and our family. Whenever Pop told the story of how Phil saved his life at D-Day, the Private always said, "I was there, so I just figured I would."

Cinque Hommes Creek coiled through the woods east of Perryville, Missouri, close to the Mississippi River. Between its curves and switchbacks, the creek attracted wildlife: wild turkeys, deer, beaver, thousands of birds, foxes, and the occasional coyote. We caught a ton of fish there—crappie, largemouth bass, channel catfish, and bluegill. I could never say which I liked better, Mom's fried chicken or her fried fish.

Pop parked his car, a blue 1948 Chevy Fleetmaster, near enough to the creek to hear it gurgle softly. The grass was lush and the trees leafed out. I opened the car door and inhaled. The air was better in the woods around the creek. It smelled better, tasted better, and made me feel excited and calm at the same time.

"I'll get the shovels," Pop said. He walked around to the back of the car and opened the trunk. You could've fit a couch in that car, but Pop drove around instead with a jumble of junk covered by an old blanket. There were two shovels, pieces of burlap cut from gunny sacks, and twine to tie up the root balls of the little trees.

I ambled around to the back of the car, stretching and sniffing. "You look like an old bear waking up from his winter hibernation," Pop laughed. He set the shovels against the fender and lifted a corner of the blanket. "What's this?" Pop said in a put-on surprise voice.

I peeked inside and spotted the butt of a shotgun. Pop pulled out a Remington 87 twelve-gauge and pretended to examine it like he never saw such a contraption in all his born days. "Hold this," he said. "Let me see what else is under this old blanket."

Pop was never as funny as he imagined, despite his devotion to Jack Benny and George Burns on Sunday evenings. He handed me a box of shotgun shells and beamed. "Happy Birthday, son." He leaned in for a hug but reconsidered when I fumbled trying to switch my new weapon from my right to my left.

"Thanks, Pop. This is perfect. Absolutely perfect."

The incongruity of a deadly weapon, with one single purpose, in this place of abundant life occurred to me for a moment. I pushed the thought aside and considered the true meaning of a shotgun. It meant manhood, and all that goes with it. On that day, I had no idea what the "all" was that went with it, but that didn't stop me from wanting to chase it down and tackle it.

"You'll notice it's a bolt action, single shot. You don't need to be laying down a spray of bullets for a rabbit or wild turkey," said Pop.

"Got it."

"Now, the rules. Rule Number One: Never use your weapon if I am not with you."

"Yes, sir."

"Rule Number Two: Never let anyone else use it, especially that knucklehead friend of yours with the bad breath."

"Calvin? Right." Calvin was a show-off and a moron. He played baseball with my best friend, Roger Pardee, who was neither of those things.

"Rule Number Three: Always look to see if anyone is ahead of you before taking your shot, even if it means you lose your prey."

"Yes, sir."

"Rule Number Four: Always carry the weapon unloaded, with the stock broke open, and the barrel pointing downward."

"Yes, sir."

"We'll keep it locked in the cabinet with mine, and I have the only key. This will help you with Rule Number One. Remember Rule Number One?"

"Yes, sir."

"All right. Let's do a little target shooting, shall we? See if this contraption works."

Pop retrieved the shotgun box from under the old blanket. On the back, Remington had printed a target. He counted out four shells into my hand and slipped a few more into his own pocket.

"One more thing," said Pop. "Do not, under any circumstances, refer to this piece as a gun or as 'Betsy.'"

"Yes, sir," I said over my shoulder as I balanced on the fallen log across Cinque Hommes Creek and into the woods.

After a few minutes walking, Pop declared that we had come to a good spot. I watched as he gathered a pile of rocks and wedged the box down among them. He turned around to face me. "No reason to shoot a perfectly good tree," he said as he walked back toward me and took up a spot just behind my right shoulder.

My hands shook a little when I loaded the piece for my first shot. Pop folded his arms to keep himself from grabbing it and loading it for me. I knew how to do it. I broke open the action, inserted a shell, closed the action, and took aim.

I fired eight shots that morning. Pop had me take two steps back for each one. I hit the target a few times. Not dead center, but nothing to be ashamed of, either. We were about to pack up to leave when Uncle Phil rolled up in a once-green pickup. He liked to say the truck was "gently rusted."

Uncle Phil was skinny and gawky. He had a loose-jointed walk that made him look unsteady or drunk, even when he was neither. Julie said he had rooster hair. When not covered by a frayed, faded St. Louis Cardinals cap, spikes of stiff brown hair stood up and out from his head. A long skinny nose, crooked smile, and a lazy way of speaking completed the picture. We who loved him understood most of what he said.

When Uncle Phil got out of his truck, I was standing like a pro with the shotgun over my forearm, the action broke open, and the barrel nose to the ground.

"I heard gunfire and I come a runnin'," Uncle Phil joked. "How did the boy do for his first time shooting?"

"The boy did pretty well with target practice. He hit the box nearly every time," Pop said.

Uncle Phil nodded his approval as he walked toward us. "Did your dad teach you the rules?"

"Yes, he did," I said.

"Good. Now, what's Rule Number 16?"

"Sixteen? Pop only gave me four rules," I said.

"That's enough rules for today," Pop said.

"You're the boss, Sarge," Uncle Phil said. He retrieved the target and scattered the rocks that held it. He then tossed it into the back of the Fleetmaster.

We followed a path into the woods before returning to the cars on the other side of Cinque Hommes Creek. I recognized the trail. I had walked it many times as Pop's unarmed assistant.

"Now, you remember the trail markings, right?"

"Sure. You showed me lots of times."

"Well, it's really important now. If something were to happen to me or to Uncle Phil, I want to make sure you can get back to the car to get help."

"You mean drive for help?" I asked much too eagerly.

"Please don't tell me you have driven a car," Pop said.

I tried not to look at Uncle Phil, but my eyes had other ideas.

"Driving's easy, kid," he said. "Have I told you I drove a

tank in the war? I can teach you the three forward gears on this old-timer in five minutes."

"I never knew you drove a tank," I said.

"Neither did I," said Pop.

"It was in Belgium, I believe. Remember we were separated for a few days?" Uncle Phil walked around us and took a position in front of Pop and me. It was his way of avoiding being asked to elaborate further.

When we got back to where the vehicles were parked, Uncle Phil said, "Let's go out to Eugene's Bear Den and celebrate Gordy's birthday. They sell soda pop, I imagine. Never ordered it myself, of course."

Pop shook his head. "We need to get home. Mom will have a lot for us to do to get ready for the party tonight."

"Well then, many happy returns. I'll head on back to the shop. I got a brake job about half done and I told the customer it would be done today." Uncle Phil opened the door of his truck and looked back at us over his shoulder. "I'm invited, ain't I?"

"Yes!" Pop called.

"Well then, to heck with the brake job. I've got to buy a birthday present for someone. Can't say any more than that."

"I wonder what his gift will be? A wrench, or maybe a pair of needle-nose pliers? I've wanted those for so long," I joked.

"Now, be nice. Your Uncle Phil loves you and Julie like his own kids. Whatever he brings, you pretend to like it, do you hear?"

"Got it, Pop."

2

PHIL

On the drive home from Gordy's "presentation of arms," I had a humdinger of an idea for the young man's birthday present. I did promise to finish a brake job at Earl's Gas 'N Go, where I worked, but to get the present I had in mind meant a good long drive. But a guy only turns fifteen once. First things first, that's what I live by.

When I arrived at Henry's place, I saw his brother-in-law Konnie's car pulled off the road. As I crossed the yard, there was Gordy, chasing his eight-year-old twin cousins with a rubber snake. Talk about boy sopranos; those twins could screech with the best of them. They ended up getting too close to each other and tumbling down onto one another. While Gordy waited with his snake to take up the chase again, I greeted everyone in the yard.

"Boys, mind your party clothes at least until we eat supper," the twins' mother called. Eileen was Ida's sister. She was also Mrs. Koenraad Veldstrom, although most everyone called her husband Konnie. Normally that would be a girl's name, but they did things differently back before the war.

People in Germany had some pretty funny names. People in France, too. But I guess "Phil Toomey" sounded pretty strange to them.

Konnie watched his boys, Jefferson and Landis, get up from the ground. Gordy had tired of the snake, and he gave it to the boys, who went looking for Julie to scare with the wiggly thing. Konnie patted Eileen's bottom and said, "Let them have some fun. I doubt Ida worries much about dirty kids, living away from town so far."

"You couldn't pay me to live out here. My sister grew up in a decent house in St. Genevieve," Eileen said, standing next to her husband in the yard.

"Don't start," said Konnie. The rivalry between Ida and her older sister ran deep. "It's Gordy's birthday, so let's just enjoy the evening for his sake."

"At least we know the cake will be good," she said. Eileen was one expert when it came to a chocolate three-layer cake.

Konnie offered me a lawn chair, and I sat down with the men. After greetings, Henry, Konnie, and me stared at the road, waiting for Jim Powell, husband of Ida's other sister Vivian, to arrive in his 1953 Buick Riviera. He drove past Konnie's car parked on the grass by the concrete slab and pulled into Henry's driveway. The rear end extended a few inches into the road. That's the Riviera's rear end, not Jim's. His wife, Vivian, was the younger sister of Ida and Eileen. She had rosy cheeks and curly blond hair; definitely the beauty of the Morrison sisters.

Jim Powell was a high school vice principal. He treated Vivian like one of his "slow" students, correcting her in front of everyone and rolling his eyes when she did something on her own. She was a sweet gal and a whiz with a needle and thread. Jim looked down his nose at me without let-up. To him, I was just a dumb old grease monkey, that is until he wanted free service on his precious Riviera.

Konnie was descended from the German abolitionists who settled in St. Louis in the 1850s. Modern Homes, his construction company in St. Genevieve, built houses, employed five men, and gave their families a turkey and case of beer each at Christmas.

When the country joined the war in 1942, Henry and I enlisted first thing. During those years, home building halted. Modern Homes did remodel work, roof repair, and plumbing, anything to keep the men working. One by one, Konnie's employees left for war. He carried on the best he could to keep the company going. One afternoon, he found his car sitting on its rims, the tires stolen, the windshield smashed, and a swastika scratched in the hood. Konnie walked home. He never squawked about his treatment during the war, just kept working at whatever jobs he could get.

Vivian carried a grocery bag of hot dog and hamburger buns into the kitchen. Jim waited until she returned to the car to retrieve her heavy crock of baked beans. He then waited some more until she was halfway to the kitchen door, pulled one bottle of beer from a six-pack in the back seat, and walked over to where we were sitting. We usually drank Schlitz, but Jim was a Miller High Life man all the way. He did not offer to share. Jim said, "Hello, boys," and pulled a *Saturday Evening Post* from his back pocket. It took him three tries to open his beer without a church key.

Jim was fifteen years older than Viv. They didn't have any kids of their own, and Vivian was the kindest, most patient lady I ever met. She would have been a dandy mom, but I heard that Jim told her, "I spend all day with snot-nosed idiots; I don't want any in my home at night as well."

Gordy's school friend, Roger Pardee, was at the party. He and Gordy played baseball together as kids. Roger was a year older than Gordy. He had already played one season on the Perryville city league, and his second season was about to start. He was a cracker-jack shortstop; never waited for the ball to come to him. That boy could turn a grounder into a double play better than most college players.

Roger didn't have many friends outside of the baseball team, though. He got burned pretty badly as a child and carried terrible scars on the back of his neck and the left side of his head. Poor kid. His daddy was killed in the Pacific,and his mother kind of gave up on life. It happened to some women who lost husbands overseas. Their kids were a daily reminder of what they had lost. It wasn't Roger's fault, but he paid the price. His house caught fire when he was only six or seven. He got burned pretty badly trying to get his drunk mother out of the house.

After being in the hospital and having skin transferred to his head from somewhere else on his body, his left ear came out shaped like a tulip. He could hear fine, thank God. But he was bald on the left side of his head. Anyway, in the lower grades, the kids made fun of him. Now he pretty much stayed to himself. Gordy was his only real friend. Roger wore a stupid plaid winter cap with flaps to cover his ears just about year-round.

After Konnie's twins got tired of the rubber snake, they borrowed Gordy's old Flying Scout skates. Henry called Julie to come out and skate with the boys. They had to take turns using Gordy's skates but managed to share pretty well. They skated on the concrete slab of the new McCann house. Julie showed her cousins how to grab the wall studs and swing themselves forward. Gordy set out three-gallon paint cans in the center of the slab to create an obstacle course.

The ladies served up a swell supper of steaks and hamburgers, potato salad, deviled eggs, baked beans, and German chocolate cake. After the meal, we adults sat under the season's new foliage on the pin oak trees. The twins amused themselves at the house across the road. Two yelping terriers ran up and down behind a chain-link fence. The boys wore themselves and the pups out. Gordy and Roger played catch until it was too dark to see the ball.

As darkness fell, Jim asked, "Is there coffee?"

I volunteered as waiter and went inside to ask Ida for some coffee. She sent me back out for a head count. As I crossed the dining room on my way back to the yard, Julie held up a little white shirt. "Look what Aunt Viv taught me to do," she said. On the tip of the right collar point was a colorful design.

"Did you draw that?" I asked.

"No, this is called embroidery. We sewed the design on with little beads," Julie boasted.

"Imagine that," I said.

After coffee was served, the ladies carried dishes inside. As laughter started up in the kitchen, Jim shouted toward the house, "Ten minutes, Vivian. Be at the car, ready to go. Not a minute later."

Ida walked to the front door and called out to her brother-in-law. "Just hold your horses. We're about to have birthday cake."

Jim stood and stretched his neck like he had been doing something strenuous. He called across the yard to his wife, "Don't forget we need to stop at the Piggly Wiggly on the way home and get you some prune juice, Vivie." He turned to me and said, "I noticed her stomach looks a little bloated. Constipation is a constant concern for our Vivie." Who says things like that about their wife at a birthday party? I may be ignorant, but I was taught manners.

Eileen stood behind Ida at the front door. She called to Konnie over Ida's shoulder, "Don't let anyone leave until every crumb of cake is gone. Henry, bring the ice cream freezer up from the basement. Gordy, show everyone your new gun. If Uncle Jim tries to leave, shoot him." Eileen pulled Ida into the house and let the screen door slam shut behind her.

Once we were full of dessert, things quieted down for the adults. The sugar had the opposite effect on the twins, of course. They were chasing lightning bugs, and the bugs were definitely winning. Us men were sprawled in chairs watching them. The women were washing dishes in the kitchen, having a gay old time by the sounds of their singing and laughing. I untangled myself from my chair and walked to my truck.

When the twins saw me coming back into the yard, they forgot all about lightning bugs. They broke into a small but loud stampede to the door of the house and yelled in one voice: "Quick, come see! Uncle Phil's outside. He brought FIREWORKS!"

We hollered for the neighbors to come over and watch the show. Julie and the ladies came outside too. I put on a pretty good show, if I say so myself. Bottle rockets and Roman candles. And I didn't forget the sparklers for the kids. Gordy and Roger helped me keep the show going. I was about as proud an uncle as if I really was Gordy's uncle. Even Jim looked up at the sky a time or two.

3

GORDY

"Tell me you did not sleep all night in this car," Pop said. He turned the key in the ignition of the Fleetmaster, but the engine failed to turn over. "Tell me you did not sit in this car all night running the radio and draining the battery."

"I slept in my bed, in pajamas, not clothes. I ate potato salad for breakfast, and I made a peanut butter and jelly sandwich for my lunch," I replied and dangled a wax paper bag containing my sandwich as Exhibit A.

Pop tried to start the car again, this time successfully. "If only you knew how to make coffee," he grumbled.

"Your thermos, My Lord," I said as I presented the red plaid cylinder of civilizing power.

"Pour, boy. Pour."

By the time Pop reached the county highway, he was alert and nearly as excited as I was for my first hunting trip with my own weapon. I cranked my head back and forth, looking out the windows as if I just landed on the planet.

"That was some party last night. Did you know Uncle Phil was bringing fireworks?"

"He said nothing, which is unusual for him. Phil is one of a kind. No one else like him on earth."

"The coolest," I affirmed.

"Be sure to thank Phil. He went to a lot of trouble and expense for you. Phil's a generous guy, but not in a showy way."

Now it was my turn to laugh. "Fireworks are pretty showy, Pop."

"Okay. I just meant he kept it to himself until the last second. Some guys would have been talking about his fireworks all afternoon, calling the neighbors to let them know. But the gift wasn't about him, so he kept it to himself."

Pop drove in silence a few miles. I reached for the radio knob, and Pop stopped me.

"Just one minute. We have to review the rules one more time."

Being the general manager of the shirt factory in town, Pop was used to giving people instructions and rules. You could say he was a pro at trying to control machines and the people who operated them.

"Yes, Pop," I answered.

"What's Rule Number One?"

"'Never let anyone else use Betsy, especially if they have bad breath,'" I repeated.

"Very funny."

"Uncle Phil asked me about Rule Number Sixteen. What's that one?"

"Rule Number Sixteen is 'Don't be disappointed if you don't

get a turkey today.' There are so many factors in hunting besides aim and shoot. It's learning about the terrain, the animals' habits, and respecting the animals. That's what I want you to remember about this day. You are part of a natural world that is complex, beautiful, and dangerous. The more you learn about it, the better you understand it, the more you'll understand what's important in your own life, and the happier you will be."

"I get it, Pop," I said as we got out of the car and walked toward the brush near the creek.

"Just give yourself a break. That's Rule Number Seventeen. I know guys who hunted wild turkeys for years before they got one," Pop whispered.

"I won't be disappointed. I just want you to be proud of me."

"Every second of every day," Pop said. "Hey, there may be times, moments, when I'm not proud of something you do. But I am always, 100% of the time, proud of the person you are and the man I know you are going to be."

Pop squeezed my shoulder. I would have liked a hug, but this seemed more appropriate. I understood, a little. I'm pretty sure Pop and I were both thinking the same thing, that we would never be the same way with each other again.

We heard a gurgling cry behind us. It was the gobble of a turkey. I looked left and right, up and down. I reached for the barrel of my shotgun to close the action.

"Hey, easy now," said Pop.

I stroked the barrel without raising it, as if I were just dusting it off a bit.

We heard the cluck again. I looked up in the trees overhead. "Sounds like a big Tom," I whispered.

Pop put his finger up to his lips. "About six feet tall, I'd say."

While I was watching the trees, Uncle Phil walked up behind me and blew his stupid turkey call right in my ear.

"I was wrong. It's not a big Tom. It's Phil," Pop said. "Late, as usual."

4

PHIL

I knew Gordy McCann since before he was born. I grew up with his dad. We went to high school together. I left school the year before Henry; he stayed to graduate. I found a job without a diploma, due to my profound knowledge of the internal combustion engine. I worked as head mechanic for Earl's Petroleum out on the highway. Earl said any goof could do oil changes and lubes, so he hired me. Being his grandson helped, I expect. I handled all the tune-ups, transmission work, plugs, brakes, and anything else that needed fixing.

Henry and I were drafted into the Army together in 1943. Henry was married by then. Gordy was still an ankle biter when we left for basic training in Biloxi. The war made us friends for life. Henry was my Sergeant, luckily. We were in the same boat on D-Day. He carried a big 50-Cal weapon. I was his spotter. The mission was clear. We were to jump into the water, locate one of the machine gun bunkers on top of the cliff, and take it out. The bunkers were easy to see thanks to the flashes of fire pouring down on the men scrambling out of boats and slogging their way onto the beach.

I gave Henry the coordinates for a bunker slightly to the right of our position. Henry rubbed the trigger lightly with his index finger, as he always did before firing. It was an old habit from our hunting trips back in Missouri. "Take a second before you pull the trigger to be certain of the target," Henry said.

That advice works well when shooting at an unarmed turkey or deer frozen still in fear. Not so much in a warzone. In that split second of hesitation, a German sniper fired. The 50-Cal flew from Henry's hands into the Channel water, taking the tip of his left thumb with it. Henry's knees buckled, and he sat down flat in the freezing water. I pulled him along beside me and ran up to the beach. Who saved whose life and how many times that day can never be calculated.

I shook my brain free of war memories when I saw Henry and Gordy ahead of me. It was chilly at Cinque Hommes Creek that day. You never knew in mid-April if it was early spring or late winter. The sun had just cleared the horizon when we reached a fallen log bridge. It would be late morning before much sun trickled down through the canopy of trees. The leaves underfoot were wet with dew and made for slippery walking.

Gordy was wearing Henry's ammo pouch from his infantry days on his belt. In it he carried his sandwich and a bottle of Coca-Cola. His shotgun was perfectly balanced over his right forearm. Henry turned as I caught up. He noticed my rifle. "No shotgun?" he asked.

"I hear at the station from hunters they are seeing lots of evidence of coyotes this year." I turned to Gordy. "Females protecting young cubs in the spring are very dangerous. I've got your back with a rifle if we do see a coyote. Just remember to keep low and keep still."

"I will. My bird shot wouldn't do much damage against that thick fur," Gordy said.

"It would irritate him some," Henry said. He opened up his trunk and selected a rifle. "I doubt we will see any coyotes, but double caution is better than ... single caution."

As we walked away from the cars, Gordy asked me, "How much is a coyote pelt worth?"

"No idea, son. There's a lot of work involved in removing a pelt so it keeps the most value."

When we reached the fallen log over the creek, I looked up into the branches of a budding sycamore. On an upper branch, I spotted a great horned owl. Henry saw him at the same time I did. He pointed up at it for Gordy.

"He's up early," Gordy whispered.

"Maybe he's just coming home late," Henry said.

I shuddered but could not speak. Seeing an owl in the daylight is bad luck. I didn't expect Henry to think of that, but I told myself to be extra careful.

I followed behind Gordy and Henry. Gordy carried his shotgun broke open across his forearm. I saw that he was holding the weapon farther away from his body than necessary. Henry didn't advise him. I started to say something but held my tongue. After twenty minutes or so, the nine-pound weapon was visibly making his shoulder tired. Gordy drew his arm in closer to his body. He's a fast learner, that boy. I was glad I held my peace.

We followed the creek at first. Henry saw a small grove of pawpaw trees, with a few purple flowers just starting to grow. "What are those trees?" Henry whispered to Gordy.

"Are they pawpaw trees?" Gordy asked.

"That's right. Long droopy leaves and flowers. Under pawpaw trees, there are bound to be lots of seeds left over from last year. They fall off the trees, and the meat of the fruit gets smashed and eaten by squirrels and birds. The seeds fall under the leaves, and in the spring, the turkeys scratch around and find them."

We stepped over to the little grove of pawpaw trees and looked at the leaves on the ground. "If the leaves look scratched up, it means turkeys have been here. What do you think, Gordy?"

"They've already been here, I'd say."

"Me, too," said Henry. "Keep your eyes open for wild strawberries. Turkeys love them, too."

"When do I look for the turkeys?" asked Gordy.

"You don't. Look for what they like to eat. They're too well camouflaged for you to see them before they get close. Best to hang back and let them come to feed," I said.

"Listen, too," Henry instructed. "Toms might be roosting up in those trees. They start moving around at first light, and you might hear a rustle or gobble overhead."

I sent out some clucks on my slate turkey call to see if any birds might come around close, in search of company for breakfast. We saw no birds in the first hour. I was hoping Gordy didn't feel let down. I tapped his shoulder. When he turned, I shrugged and pointed ahead. Gordy understood that I meant "Don't get discouraged. Maybe we'll have better luck up ahead."

I heard the ground leaves rustling. Henry stopped and put out his right arm to block Gordy, like parents do. Gordy held himself completely still. Henry signaled for Gordy to get down slowly behind some brush in front of us. We heard cries from an animal in a small clearing ahead.

I raised up as tall as I could to see what was causing all the racket. A she coyote stepped out from behind a tree, shaking a red fox kit pinned between her powerful jaws. Approaching her was a vixen, the kit's mother. She took a step and barked in alarm. The coyote stared at her, still holding her dead baby between her teeth.

The vixen walked slowly backward, toward the brush where Gordy was huddled. The coyote continued to watch her and dropped the dead kit onto the ground. I breathed slowly. Henry drew his weapon into firing position, inch by inch.

A tiny, high-pitched yap cut through the tension. It came from in front of where Gordy was crouching. Another fox kit. The den must have been right in front of Gordy. The coyote heard the cry and turned abruptly in its direction. The vixen stopped her backward crawl. I raised my weapon and turned my head a few degrees left and right, looking for signs of another coyote.

Another cry, more urgent, came from the den. The vixen set herself to charge the coyote if she moved forward. Henry and I were in position to fire if the coyote did not turn away. We were trained to wait for the best shot. I heard a stirring near Gordy. And that's when I saw him. He was crawling toward the den. He wanted to save the crying kit. He probably thought the coyote's attention on the vixen gave him an opportunity. But no such luck. The coyote sensed the movement. I saw the muscle in her right flank ripple.

I lined up a shot at the coyote's head. I felt a tiny movement in the air between us when Henry prepared to shoot. Gordy had to crawl over some fallen branches to get to the den. He raised up to get over them. In the same heartbeat, Gordy jumped toward the den, the coyote jumped toward him, and Henry and I fired our weapons. The coyote dropped, shot in the head. The vixen ran into the brush behind us.

When the coyote sprang for the den, Henry and I fired two high-velocity, .22 caliber bullets. Our rifle barrels nearly touched as we fired together. I am a half-inch taller than Henry. At some point, the bullets must have moved into the same tunnel of air, one on top of the other. See, a bullet moves in flight. The yaw motion is the bullet wobbling up and down along a horizontal trajectory. Two bullets, their paths scarcely an inch apart, traveling over 2,000 feet per second. The air channel of one bullet affected the flight of the other, so that one fell a microscopic distance in its path. The bullet on the upper track hit the coyote. The other bullet entered Gordy's body below his left arm.

5

GORDY

"I fell, Pop."

"Hush, son. Stay still."

"Fell on a sharp stick. My chest hurts."

Pop lifted my left arm. There was a small, round hole in my sweater.

Uncle Phil ran forward to make sure the coyote was dead. He looked through the sight of his rifle, ready to shoot again if necessary. When he kicked the coyote, its head flopped. Then he lowered his weapon.

"Did I shoot myself?" I cried.

"No, son. It was an accident."

Uncle Phil came back to where I was lying. He hung his rifle over his shoulder and bent down close to me. I heard Pop say, "No exit wound. Go get your truck. I'll keep him quiet."

"Can't get the truck all the way in here. Let's carry him up a ways, and I'll run for the truck."

Uncle Phil and Pop locked their arms to make a carrier seat. Neither one suggested it. Their training took over.

"You just lay back and we'll do all the work," Uncle Phil said. "We'll get you out of here quick, right Sarge?"

"Right. Just go limp, son. Relax, and we'll give you the gentlest ride we can. It's not far."

The men walked carefully in step to keep me from bumping around and moving the bullet that was still inside me. The distance to the clearing was no more than a quarter mile.

When they laid me down under some cottonwood trees, I thought they had put me on a fire. My chest and back burned something fierce. Pop rolled up my jacket for a pillow. Was this why he wanted me to bring it? Bring it where? I was confused. Pop covered me with Uncle Phil's big jacket. Where did he go?

"Uncle Phil?"

"He's bringing his truck. We have to take you to the doctor," Pop said.

I slept a minute, I guess. When I woke up, Pop was sitting next to me, holding my arms across my chest. There was a little window over our heads, but I don't think it was a building. Pop yelled through the little window, "Get this fucker moving." He looked at me and said, "You will be all right. I'll hold onto you."

I saw trees with little green leaves over my head. The branches were sliding away. The sunlight flickered through the trees. It made me dizzy. Then, the trees disappeared. I thought a blue blanket covered me, and on the blanket were white, fluffy animals. *Did I have a blanket like that when I was a baby? Am I a baby now?* I wondered.

"The bed is moving, Pop," I said.

"We are in a truck. In the back. See the beautiful sky over us?"

The sky. Of course. I started to remember. "The baby fox?"

"He's safe in his den. His mama is taking care of him."

"Am I shot?" I asked.

"Yes, son. We are taking you to the hospital." Pop lifted my shirt. Then he pressed on my belly. "Internal bleeding," he said.

A drop of water fell on my face from the sky. It rolled onto my lips and tasted salty. Pop wiped it away. Before I fell asleep again, more drops fell on me. Rain from a blue blanket of sky? I did not understand at all. The next time I woke up, I was on the sun. A light so bright over me that I couldn't see anything else. My clothes were all burned off, too. Also, my legs were gone. I slept a long time.

6

PHIL

We took Gordy to the Perry County Memorial Hospital. It was a small hospital but close. The Emergency Department had two treatment rooms and one operating room. Dr. Aiken was in charge that day. His E.R. treated mostly children with earaches or men who stepped on a nail or cut off a fingertip with a circular saw. However, Dr. Aiken was a corpsman in the war and had seen plenty of gunshot wounds. When he came home, he studied medicine in St. Louis and served his residency at the Veterans' Hospital at Jefferson Barracks. All to say, Dr. Aiken knew spinal cord injuries, and he knew he was looking at one in the trauma bay that Sunday morning.

The x-rays told the whole story. The bullet entered from the back, at the 6th rib on the left side. The rib was cracked, but no pieces had broken off. There was a lot of blood in the abdomen. Some organ had been hit.

"Prep the O.R., stat," Dr. Aiken ordered the nurse. "Call St. Anthony's and alert them we're sending an SCI as soon as he's stable. Arrange an ambulance. In that order."

Dr. Aiken ran into Henry on his way to scrub for surgery. "We need to operate and find out the source of his internal bleeding. Once he's stabilized, he's going to St. Anthony's. They have more experience than any place in the Midwest with spinal cord injuries. Wait here. I'll talk to you when we're done."

St. Anthony's Hospital in St. Louis was more than sixty miles away. It was world-famous for treating patients in the polio epidemic of 1949. The hospital specialized in children who could not walk. Henry knew this. When the doc mentioned St. Anthony's, Henry's knees buckled. He leaned against the wall outside the operating room. He could not catch his breath.

"Sit down, buddy. Don't anticipate. Wait and see," I said.

"I have to call Ida." Henry choked out the words.

"Already done. I called Earl, and he is going to pick up Ida and Julie."

"Julie?"

"Can't leave her home alone. Earl and me will keep her occupied," I promised.

"What did you tell Ida?"

"Just that there was an accident. We brought Gordy here to get him checked out. That's it. It's the truth, and it's all we know right now."

I wrangled Henry down a green-tiled corridor to a little meeting room and turned on the light. "This looks okay. Sit tight, Sarge. I'll find us some coffee and tell the nurse where we are. She'll bring Ida when she gets here."

Henry walked around the little table, looked out the window at the parking lot, and then circled again. I stayed out of his way. He sat down and held his head between his hands like he expected it might explode.

"I shot my son. He may die."

"Come on, now. He was awake when we brought him in," I

said. The pale green of the tile walls turned my stomach. Sea Foam Green, it was called. I had seen it on paint sample cards. I thought Henry was going to lose his cookies.

"Phil, we've seen this before, in Belgium. Remember? Guys not much older than Gordy shot up, crippled, worse."

"Hold up." I treated the sarge the same way he handled wounded in Belgium. Or, at least I tried. "Those were big caliber automatic weapons we were using. Combat conditions. Dirt, smoke. Gordy's in a clean place with good people, good equipment."

I turned to leave the room but was blocked by the Perry County sheriff. Walter Guillaume (which he pronounced "Gillum") had been elected sheriff of Perry County four times. He descended from an old St. Louis French family.

"Mr. McCann, I'd like to ask you a few questions."

I held my place at the door, between Henry and the sheriff. He turned to me and said, "I thought I heard you say something about coffee."

I did not want Henry to talk to the law in his condition. He might get flustered and say something he shouldn't, something he didn't know yet. I stepped back into the hall just to the right of the door. The sun was in front of me, so I wouldn't cast a shadow under the door. Old soldier's trick from fighting in bombed-out buildings.

Sheriff Guillaume closed the door. I caught a nurse's attention and gestured for two coffees. She nodded and walked back in the direction she had come. I heard the sound of one chair scraping the floor. The sheriff was likely standing, so Henry had to look up at him. I heard the conversation through the open transom overhead.Thank God for old buildings.

"What happened out there?"

"We were hunting turkeys. Saw a coyote. Phil and I fired at the coyote. Gordy jumped in the way and was hit."

"Why would he jump in front of you firing?"

"He was distracted, I guess. The coyote had killed one kit and was headed toward the den for another. Gordy was on the ground behind some brush. He tried to reach into the den and rose up enough for the coyote to attack. We both fired at the same time. The coyote was a bitch. A big one."

"So, just an accident?"

"Of course, it was an accident. That's my son in there being cut on." Henry was seconds away from grabbing something, anything, and throwing it at someone, anyone.

"I understand. I have to investigate. Even accidents. Did you scare off the coyote?" the sheriff asked.

"Killed her."

"Good for you. Too many of those damned things around here."

The nurse returned with two coffees in thick dinner mugs. I knocked on the door. No one said "come in," but I went in anyway. I set one coffee in front of Henry and offered the second cup to the sheriff. He waved the cup away with a flash of a smile. I set the mug on the table and left the room. In the hallway, I made a few steps in place so the sheriff would think I was walking away. I must have convinced him because his next question to Henry was, "Now, which one of you hit the coyote and which one hit the boy?"

I could hear Henry's voice tightening with every word. "We fired at the same time."

"You and your friend were in the war together, right? Infantry?"

"Third Army," Henry mumbled.

"Patton's boys."

"I never saw the man."

"Died a while back, didn't he? Car accident, I read. Injured his spine."

There was a long pause. I knew Henry was in there picking at his cuticles. They were likely bleeding by now. It's what he did, but not a good thing to do in front of a suspicious sheriff. The sheriff continued, "If you and your friend fired at the exact same time, we'll have to recover the bullets and run ballistics to see who did what."

"Why?"

"For the reports." Sheriff Guillaume did not speak for a minute. Probably getting his little notebook to write down the ammunition information.

Hold it together, Sarge, I thought.

"Now, what ammo do you use?"

"Me? I use Federal .22 Cal, 40g."

"That's high velocity for turkeys," the sheriff said.

I heard Henry's hands slap against the tabletop. "Gordy was hunting turkeys. Phil and I were watching for coyotes."

"Well, Dr. Aiken will give me anything he removes from your son. That leaves the coyote. Your friend can go with me and show me the scene. I'll recover the carcass and we'll see what's inside. Then, we'll know who shot what."

"And if the bullet in Gordy came from my gun?" Henry asked.

"My report will so reflect."

"It was an accident," Henry growled.

"Even accidents get reported. Big part of my job."

I heard the chair scrape again. Henry was up and pacing now.

"Who has access to this report?" Henry asked.

"Anyone. Insurance companies are usually the most interested. It's public record, Mr. McCann."

I pushed the door open with my shoulder and stepped into the room. The sheriff saw me but did not look surprised. He looked at me but spoke to Henry. "What's your friend's name?"

"I'm Phil Toomey," I said. "Any chance you could leave this man alone? I was there. I can tell you whatever you need to write in your notebook."

Henry picked up a coffee mug from the table. His hand was shaking. I stepped toward the door and said, "I'm as ready as I can get, sheriff. Let's go find a dead coyote."

"Big one, was it?"

I stared at the sheriff's forehead so as to not make eye contact. "Looked mighty big to me, sir," I said.

I let Sheriff Guillaume go through the door first. He put on his hat, positioning it just so to his liking. I turned back to Henry and asked, "You okay, Sarge? I can put off that sheriff. Say the word."

"Remember the English Channel? Before dawn. Water black as week-old coffee, cold as the dead floating in it."

"How can I forget? But we made it through."

"Gordy's not a soldier. He's a boy, a child, a baby."

I followed the sheriff down the corridor. He turned back to me and said, "Well, at least the chickens of Perry County can sleep well tonight."

As we got close to the lobby, I heard Ida's voice at the reception desk.

"Ida McCann, here for Gordon Michael McCann," she said. Ida became officious when she was afraid. Earl was sitting in a chair, awaiting orders. Julie stood behind her mother, eyes as big as silver dollars.

"I'll meet you in a minute," I said to the sheriff.

"Take your time," he said. He went out the door toward his squad car.

The nurse had come out from behind the reception desk. "This way," she said to Ida.

I fell in behind Ida and the nurse. Poor Julie tiptoed along behind Ida. She kept her eyes toward the floor. The sound of all our eight feet walking out of step clattered in the hallway. The nurse opened the door of the little room where Henry waited. He was standing behind his chair, frozen. Julie tried to run to her father, but Ida held her back. She looked around the tiny room and turned to face the nurse.

"Where's my son? He's not here. I said I wanted to be taken to my son. Gordon Michael Morrison." Ida used her maiden name. She was declaring Gordy her child, hers alone. No one was to claim him or touch him without her permission. Whatever Henry had done or said was now overturned, overruled.

"He's still in surgery, Ida," Henry whispered.

"Is that right?" Ida asked the nurse.

"Yes, ma'am. Dr. Aiken will speak to you as soon as he is finished."

Ida thanked the nurse and pushed Julie in her direction. "Go back to the lobby, honey. Uncle Jim and Aunt Viv are on their way. They'll take you home with them later." Julie gave Henry a weak wave and let the nurse turn her around toward the door.

Ida looked at me like I was trying to horn in on a family matter. "Why don't you sit with Julie? The sheriff is waiting out there. I don't want her to be more scared than she already is."

I nodded in obedience, but I was not yet dismissed. Ida turned to the nurse as she left and said, "Julie is Gordon's sister. My sister and her husband are coming to take her home with them. In the meantime, if you can find some paper for Julie to draw on, I would be very grateful."

"Yes, ma'am. We've got crayons and lots of drawing paper. I know where to find some graham crackers, too."

The nurse left with Julie, pulling the door closed behind her. I intended to catch up with them, but something told me to stay a beat longer. Ida didn't ask me to leave. Instead, she squared off with me and demanded, "Did you shoot my son?"

"We both shot at the same time," I said.

"Two shots?!"

I talked as fast as I could muster. "Only one hit Gordy. The other bullet hit a coyote that was about to attack Gordy. We dropped the coyote before she could hurt him."

"So, one bullet in the coyote and one in my boy. Which of you missed the coyote?"

"We don't know," Henry said.

"Why not?" Ida insisted.

Henry dropped his head into his arms on the table. He was spent.

I answered for Sarge, "The bullets are still in the bodies, ma'am."

"Bodies?" Ida screamed.

Henry raised his head. His face was distorted with sobbing. "The dead coyote's body and Gordy's very much alive body."

"Why is he in surgery?" Ida asked him. She brushed his hair tenderly.

"There was internal bleeding. Once he's stabilized, he'll be transferred to St. Anthony's Hospital," I said.

I pulled up a chair beside Henry. Ida fell into it. She was not ready to weep, but she had used up her angerfor the present. She looked into her husband's face and saw her own helplessness mirrored back.

Henry clasped Ida's hands and spoke softly. "I've seen this before in the war, honey. The x-ray showed no broken ribs. His heart was not hit, nor his lungs. The doctors at St. Anthony's specialize in this kind of injury. The doctor here, Dr. Aiken, seems experienced, and he's got a big heart. He'll do all he can for your baby."

I stood by the one window in the little room and looked out at the parking lot. Sheriff Guillaume was smoking a cigarette by his car. He did not look mad—yet.

I heard Ida behind me. "Henry, just tell me one thing: was Phil drunk?"

I put my right hand over my heart. "I never drink when I hunt," I declared. "Especially with a kid. Even more especially with Gordy."

Henry had calmed himself a little. He stood close to Ida and took her hands in his. "Phil was trying to kill the coyote before it jumped Gordy, same as me. He handled Gordy so gently when we carried him to the truck."

I walked on tiptoe toward the waiting room door.

"Where are you off to?" Ida asked.

"Back to the woods. The sheriff is here. I've got to go with him to recover the coyote."

Ida did not seem to understand. There was so much coming at her too fast.

"Why?" she shouted.

"For the bullet."

Ida nodded. She let go of Henry's hands and picked up the coffee mug on the table. The coffee was stone cold by now. Her hand shook, so she could not hold it still. Henry took the cup from her and helped her sit down. She stared at a wall across the room. "What a disgusting shade of green," she muttered. I waited for a nod from the sarge and hustled out to meet the sheriff.

7

DR. DREESEN

When I got the call from Dr. Aiken in Perryville, he was just going into surgery with Gordy. "I'll mop up the internal bleeding and get the boy stabilized. Then, he's all yours."

"Thanks for the heads-up. Call me when he's on the way. In the meantime, have a nurse call me and describe the x-rays. You get scrubbed."

I did not want to keep the doctor talking. A nurse called later. "Dr. Aiken is still in surgery. No major organs were damaged. Spleen laceration caused the bleeding. Dr. Aiken has cleaned it out. When the patient wakes up, we'll send him your way. Nice young man."

"How old is the patient?" I asked.

"Just turned fifteen. Otherwise good health. Nice parents. What a shame."

It's always a shame, I thought.

I chose spinal cord injuries as my emphasis when I worked under a great mentor. It happens that way often with medical students. I volunteered for the Army in 1944. I did my residency at City Hospital of Boston, studying under Dr. Donald Munro, the "pioneer in optimism." Dr. Munro began neurosurgical treatment of spinal cord injuries in World War I. Back then, spinal injuries carried an 80% mortality rate. Dr. Munro believed that successful treatment of these patients was possible and worthwhile. He focused on preventing complications, controlling spasms, and facilitating rehabilitation.

Gordy and his family arrived later that day. Unfortunately, I had seen this before: a gurney carrying a young patient, the attendants buzzing around the patient's head. They moved at a professional trot: walking fast but not running so as not to alarm the family. The parents scurried behind, eyes red from crying and wide with fear. I stepped toward them and looked at the patient's face for signs of shock. Kids make the best patients because they generally do what is asked of them without question. Parents, however, require special handling. They love their child but hate the world for doing mischief to him. They withhold judgment on the doctor until they see what he can do.

8

PHIL

In the squad car, I told the sheriff, "I know it was my bullet that hit Gordy. I'm guilty. It was an accident, but I still did it. Henry was always the better shot. He shot the coyote. No doubt in my mind. Even if it turns out that it wasn't my bullet, just go ahead and say that it was. You want me to swear? I will. You want me to write a confession? Just hand over some paper and a pen."

Sheriff Guillaume understood what he was hearing: a desperate man trying to save a dear friend. "I hear you. I'll wait for the report to corroborate."

I admit that I was relieved to be away from the hospital. *That's all family business now,* I told myself. *They'll need my help later, and I'll be ready.*

"This about the place?" the sheriff asked.

"Yes, sir. We parked just up a-ways. Here are the tire tracks from where I drove down to get Gordy."

We followed the fresh tire tracks into the woods and parked next to Henry's Fleetmaster. From where the tracks ended, it was no more than a five-minute walk to the fox den. I checked the den. It was empty.

"I guess the kit is out there somewhere, alone," I said.

"So, where were you and Mr. McCann standing?"

"Right over there. Gordy made a grab for the kit crying down in the den. It caught the coyote's attention. She should be right over there."

But there wasn't a coyote's body anywhere nearby. I looked left and right. "She must have got up after we left and then wandered off to die."

The sheriff leaned down and examined the grass. There was a trail of broken blades where the coyote seemed to have been dragged away. Lots of blood, too.

"Yep, this is where the coyote went down," said Sheriff Guillaume. "We're standing in its blood. Somebody got a free coyote pelt."

The sheriff shoved the tarp under his arm and walked back the way we'd come.

I ran to catch up with him. "How are we going to know whose bullet hit Gordy?"

"We've got another bullet to examine," he said.

***

Henry's car was still parked at Cinque Hommes Creek. The sheriff offered me a ride to the hospital to get my truck. "Thanks anyway, but Henry gave me his keys, so I'll just drive his car back and leave it there for him."

I floored that Fleetmaster all the way to the hospital just as they were loading Gordy into the ambulance. Vivian and Jim Powell had arrived by then. They would follow the ambulance to St. Louis with Julie. I offered to drive Henry and Ida behind the ambulance.

"I'm riding with Gordy," Ida said. "Henry?"

"Thanks for bringing the car. I want to stay with Gordy. It's up to you if you want to go to the hospital. You can ride with Julie. She's going with Jim and Viv."

There wasn't a chance of that happening. "How about I drive the Fleetmaster so you'll have it to go home when you're ready?" Henry nodded.

"I can call Earl to pick me up at St. Anthony's after he closes. He'll curse a good while, but he'll come."

I walked past my truck. It was a mess. Earl would bring me back for it. I wanted to get it home and clean up the blood in the back. Give me something to think about besides whose bullet hit Gordy. For now, I joined the procession of ambulance, Jim's car, and Fleetmaster to St. Anthony's Hospital.

I lost the ambulance at St. Genevieve. It cut over to Butler Hill Road and picked up Highway 21. They were moving with lights and sirens, of course. When I arrived at St. Anthony's, I saw the ambulance parked near the emergency room door. The back door was open, and the attendants were having a smoke. Jim's car was in the parking lot.

I walked over to the ambulance and bummed a smoke from one of the guys. "How's the kid doing?" I asked.

"Are you with the family?" they asked.

"Sometimes," I said. I guess I was feeling a little left out. Gordy was as close to a son as I was going to get.

"He was fine when we dropped him off."

I tossed my cigarette butt and headed for the door. I couldn't go inside through the ambulance entrance, so I shoved my hands down hard in my pockets and walked to the visitor's entrance. *I'm as much of an uncle to Gordy as Jim Almighty Powell*, I thought.

A nun was sitting behind the reception desk. She smiled and pointed toward the big coffee urn in the reception area. I walked over and filled up a cup with about equal parts coffee and sugar.

I turned to face Jim and Viv. "Anyone want coffee?" I asked from the little table.

"No, thanks," Jim said. He lifted a cup to show me he had found the coffee already, then went back to flipping the pages of a magazine. He frowned like he was grading a third grader's spelling test, and it was real bad.

"The medical world sure pushes the coffee," I said with a weak chuckle. Only Viv looked at me and smiled. Julie ran across the room and grabbed my free hand. She pulled me down to her level to whisper to me. "Did you find the baby fox?"

"No, sweetheart. It must have run off with all the noise and confusion."

"But how will it live without its mother?"

"I'm pretty sure I spotted another den when we carried Gordy to the truck. I expect the kit went there and has already been adopted. Tell you what, tomorrow morning, I'll drive out and check on him. I bet I'll find him playing with his new brothers and sisters."

Julie returned to repeat my story to Viv, who nodded her head in agreement.

After a few minutes, the nun brought Henry and Ida to the waiting room. Ida reported that Dr. Dreesen was examining Gordy and that he was a spine specialist.

I rose and gave my seat to Ida. I knew I was the skunk at the picnic as far as she was concerned, but I would have to suck it up for Henry and Gordy. The air in the room seemed to be swirling overhead, like a storm cloud forming. Probably all the prayers going up from all of us stirred it.

9

DR. DREESEN

The page came when I was just sitting down to a late lunch in St. Anthony's cafeteria. Salisbury steak. "Dr. Dreesen, report to ER stat." I scraped the gravy off the hamburger patty, carried my tray around the counter to the grill, grabbed two pieces of bread from the open loaf next to a toaster, and ran out the door two bites into my sandwich.

As a physician, I would never approve of eating a hamburger while running, but there I was. As I entered the ER, I tossed what was left of my sandwich in a trash can and force-swallowed what remained in my mouth.

In the treatment room, I washed my hands and verified that the patient from Perryville had arrived. "GSW, male, age 15. Stable. Probable SCI." I was pulling a fresh gown from the cabinet as I heard the siren as it pulled off Highway 21.

Gordy's parents had accompanied him in the ambulance. His father rode up front, and his mother in back with a medic. My patient was conscious but sedated. The medics wheeled him into a treatment room for vitals before admission.

Outside the treatment room, Mr. McCann offered his hand. "This is Gordy. It was a hunting accident."

"Dr. Alger Dreesen. After I take a look at Gordy, I'll come and talk to you. Sister Alison will show you where to wait. If you need anything, feel free to ask her."

I left Mr. and Mrs. McCann confused and frightened outside the curtained treatment area. From there on, the nurses were responsible for their needs. The medics had already transferred Gordy to an examination table.

When my initial examination was finished and Gordy was on his way to a room, I found his parents along with some family members in the reception area.

Mrs. McCann rose from her chair. "You're finished?"

"I've had a good look at Gordy's x-rays. No major organ damage at all. That's good news. Dr. Aiken cleaned up the bleeding from the lacerated spleen. Gordy is not hemorrhaging at this time. We will watch him carefully for a few weeks, but I don't expect any complications. For now, we will monitor his incision for any signs of infection. Keep him turned so he doesn't develop pressure sores. Once the wound is healing well, we'll start rehabilitation and get Gordy home as soon as possible. We all recover better in familiar surroundings, with family."

I had been lucky to study with Dr. Munro during the war. He taught us to exude optimism to the patient and family even before all the facts were known. I agree with him in terms of patient care. Optimism leads a physician to explore many options. But my experience with parents of young patients is that they take everything doctors say as gospel. If something changes, as it can and often does, they become angry. I would, too.

"Gordy has been admitted. His room is on the third floor, room 312."

"Can we see him?" Mrs. McCann asked. She was already looking over my shoulder toward the empty treatment room. I knew they had urgent questions.

"The floor nurse will need a few minutes to get Gordy settled in his room. You will be more comfortable in my office. I am glad to answer any questions you have. Just keep in mind that it's early days in Gordy's recovery."

I didn't want to sit behind a desk. Too officious. So I pulled my chair out from behind my desk and sat beside them. "When you say rehabilitation, what exactly do you mean?" Mrs. McCann asked.

"Physical therapy."

Mr. McCann said, "Right after he was injured, Gordy said he could not feel his legs."

"Your son sustained a spinal cord injury. There is a lot of swelling from the trauma of the injury. We can't tell if he will recover the use of his legs."

Mrs. McCann began to cry. "Dr. Aiken said nothing about not walking."

"We will do everything we can. Gordy is in good health and young. He is in a good place at St. Anthony's. We'll take good care of him."

Mr. McCann leaned toward his wife and reached for her hand. She did not take his. "When will you operate?" she asked.

"They operated in Perryville. Did a nice job, too. The spleen was only nicked, so it did not have to be removed. They stopped the bleeding, checked out the surrounding organs, which are fine. Spinal cord injuries are my specialty. I served in the Army during the war. I saw a lot of boys not much older than Gordy."

"Boys who can't walk now?" asked Mr. McCann.

"Boys who have useful lives. Boys who have learned to use the abilities they have to the fullest. Wheelchairs, braces, or crutches do the rest. Ninety percent of patients with injuries like Gordy's survive now."

Mrs. McCann was breathing in gasps, trying to calm down. Mr. McCann put his arm around her shoulder. This time, she allowed it.

"This is a lot to absorb, I know. Gordy will need some time just to heal from the insult to his body. The bullet moved almost completely through his chest."

"Did the bullet go through his spine?" asked Mr. McCann.

"Oh, no. The spinal cord is not severed. His injury is what we call an incomplete spinal cord injury. The concussion of the bullet inside the body caused the spinal cord to turn soft at about T-3. That's good news because damage lower in the spine would mean problems with bladder and bowel and sexual function. There is a good chance those functions will return. Of course, he is catheterized for now."

I paused. This was too much information, but patients are often relieved to hear medical jargon. It gives them a feeling of confidence in the provider. Also, they needed to know, to be partners in their son's recovery.

"So, if the bullet isn't in his spine, where is it?" Mrs. McCann asked.

I held up an x-ray toward the overhead light. "The bullet is this small dark spot near the end of this rib."

"I thought you said you did not plan to operate," she said.

"There is no need to take it out. It's snug there under the rib."

Mrs. McCann's eyes narrowed into slits. "What if it goes into his lungs or his heart?"

"Very rare for a projectile to move. Even if it did, it couldn't penetrate an organ. It is inside the rib cage."

"Won't the metal rust in there? Poison Gordy? I've heard of lead poisoning before," she insisted.

"Entirely different," I said.

Mr. McCann looked panicked. "You have to remove the bullet. We need it."

"For what?"

"I don't want a bullet in my son's body," Mrs. McCann cried.

"There's no medical reason to remove it." I extended my hand to Mrs. McCann. "Let's go see your son now."

As we waited for the elevator, Mr. McCann inhaled until he could hold no more air. "There might be other reasons to remove the bullet," he said quietly.

"There's no medical reason to remove it, so performing such a surgery would be exposing Gordy to unnecessary risk. Infection, even death. It would be malpractice."

After a long pause, Mr. McCann said, "The bullet is evidence, don't you see?"

"Evidence of what?"

"Evidence of who shot Gordy, my friend or me. We both fired at a coyote at the same time. One of us killed the animal."

"I see. You should talk to the police about that. Otherwise, Mr. McCann, you will have to find a way to live with the odds that the bullet was yours. Fifty-fifty may be the best answer you're going to get. Let's go and see Gordy, shall we?"

The old elevator clunked when it came to rest in front of us. I held the door for the McCanns. "We have a chaplain if you would like to talk to him about non-medical matters. Religious or not, he's a good man to talk to. Let me take care of Gordy for now."

Mrs. McCann was still blotting her face with a handkerchief. "Doctor, how much does Gordy know?"

"He knows he's going to survive and get well. That's enough for now," I said. I was parroting my mentor, Dr. Munro. He used to talk to me about my bedside manner. The practice of medicine is part science, part compassion," he said.

"Imagine Tarzan swinging through the jungle on vines; first a vine of sober science and then catching a vine of empathic compassion—with Jane on your back and the chimp sitting on your head."

10

PHIL

St. Anthony's Hospital sat smack in the middle of a square block in South St. Louis. That made it pretty easy to find. I went for coffee after checking in on everyone in the lobby. I figured the family would be talking with the doctors, which was none of my business. When I returned, the ambulance was gone. I decided I had waited long enough, so I parked Henry's car on Chippewa Avenue and walked up the wide curved driveway to the entrance. The driveway ran the whole length of Chippewa Avenue from South Grand to Arkansas Avenue. The building was red brick, just like all the buildings and houses around it. They built them to last back in those days.

The entrance for visitors was under a sort of brick canopy. Inside, I thought I was in some grand hotel you might see in a movie. To the right was an enormous white marble half-wall. Several ladies worked behind the wall at wooden desks. Some were nurses in white dresses and caps. Others were nuns in full-dress habits.

"Hello, how may I help you, sir?" one of the sisters asked in a cheerful voice.

"I'm here to see a patient, well not necessarily him, but his parents. But also the patient. His name is Gordy McCann." I was glad that nuns have to practice forgiveness because I sounded like a stuttering fool. I glanced over my shoulder to the large waiting area and spotted Jim Powell.

"McCann? Let me take a look," said Sister Alison.

I looked back toward the clusters of comfortable chairs with padded arms and low tables with small lamps. I saw Vivian and Julie. They sat on a loveseat with their heads together over a sewing project. Jim was standing behind them, waving his right arm at me and pointing to his head. Then he made a gesture like he was taking off a hat. I understood. I was wearing my Earl's Gas and Garage cap. I grabbed the bill of it and yanked it off. I was smoothing my uncombed hair when Sister Alison returned.

Sister Alison asked if I wanted her to take me to Gordy's room. I said, "Yes, please. Let me talk with these people first. That's the patient's aunt and uncle. The little girl is his sister, Julie."

"Just let me know when you're ready," Sister Alison said.

As soon as I said, "Howdy," Jim complained about driving all the way into the city. "Julie insisted on seeing Gordy. I understand her anxiety, not knowing what is going on. None of us really know, do we?"

"Thanks for bringing her," I said. "If she sees him with her own eyes, she'll believe he's alive and going to get better."

Jim agreed, I guess. He shrugged and said, "It's just basic psychology, really."

He meant it as a jab at dumb Phil Toomey, but I didn't care if a jackass talked bad about me. I asked Julie if she was hungry and offered to locate some ice cream for her. Viv thought it was a terrific idea, and the three of us walked to the reception desk to ask where we might find ice cream at this hour. The sister said the cafeteria had an ice cream machine and called to make sure someone was there to serve us. We left Jim alone in the lobby. What an ass.

The three of us took the stairs down to the first floor. In the privacy of the stairwell, Julie asked us, "Do you think Gordy will die?"

"Oh no. The doctor said he's going to heal up just fine. Hey, you can be his little nurse when he gets home," Viv said. "I'll make you a white apron like the sisters wear."

"No, Mom will do everything for him."

"Why do you say that?" I asked.

"Because Gordy is her favorite. Mom always cooks what he likes."

"What is your favorite supper?" I asked.

"I like green beans and new potatoes. With lots of butter," Julie said.

"Me, too," I said, rubbing my beer belly.

"But Mom doesn't cook them, even when I ask her to. Daddy and Gordy like green beans cooked with red onions, and Mom doesn't have time to make two kinds for one meal."

"I see."

"Onions make the green beans stinky, but Gordy likes them, so it's onions every day," Julie said.

"Every day?"

"Seems like. If Gordy is listening to baseball on the radio, I can't watch television. Gordy gets to go off by himself to play baseball or ride his bike to the park. He goes to the hardware store with Pop."

"Do you like to go to the hardware store?" I asked.

"Well, not much. I do like to play with the levels. I try to get all the bubbles in the middle at one time. It's harder than you think."

I laughed. I realized I was guilty of ignoring Julie. But never Ida, never Henry.

Viv brushed Julie's curls behind her ears. "It may seem like Gordy is your mom's favorite, but I happen to remember how happy she was when her beautiful daughter was born."

"Well, Mom does lots of things for me, too. It's just those stinky onions I really hate," Julie said.

I ordered vanilla ice cream cones for the three of us. Julie smiled a few times. I guess I had a good idea for once.

When we returned from our "outing," I found Sister Alison and told her I was ready to go up to Gordy's room. We rode a steel cage elevator up to the third floor. When we stopped, the Sister jerked on the elevator's heavy door like a champ. When I stepped out, she smiled and pointed to the right. "Room 312, just down this hall."

"Thank you," I said. I looked down at my dirty hands, shoved them in my pockets, and turned to the left. At the end of the hall, I saw Henry standing in front of a large window. He was smoking a cigarette with his back to the hallway. I headed his way, content he knew where Gordy's room would be.

Henry smoked some in the Army. We all did. The government packed cigarettes in every box of rations. Two cigarettes in a little pack. We smoked together, relaxing after a march or a meal. A burning butt could warm a guy's face and fingers in the cold. The slight buzz from a cigarette could wake a guy up or settle him for sleep on the ground. It even silenced a stomach screaming with hunger when a guy had been under fire for hours on end.

Henry heard me and turned toward the hallway. His greeting to me was, "Tuck in your shirt tail, for God's sake."

Anything to please the sarge, I looked down at my shirt. The tail was hanging out, and there were a few dark red spots near a missing button at the end. It had to be Gordy's blood. There had not been much, even when we loaded him into the back of the truck. I jammed as much of my shirt as I could into my pants.

Henry led me to a set of doors that opened to a small balcony. The dusk breeze was cool and felt good on my bare head. Henry lit a new cigarette without offering me one. The south side of St. Louis spread out before us. Lights were starting to appear here and there on the upper floors of the buildings down below. I leaned out over the balcony railing and turned my head as far as I could. "I thought we might see the river from here."

"We're too far to see it," Henry said.

He stubbed out his second cigarette since VE Day in a planter at the edge of the balcony. The dry stems of chrysanthemums from last fall were brittle, and scraps of the blossoms crumbled when the breeze picked up. It was still early to plant spring flowers.

"Ida will have my hide if she smells smoke on my clothes," he said.

"I doubt she will notice under the circumstances."

I wanted to say a word or two that might help Henry in the days ahead. I couldn't think of a single positive thing to say except, "At least Gordy's alive."

After a good while, Henry sighed and said, "I've been standing here thinking about some of the things Gordy will never do. He can't go down the stairs at home or leave the house alone. Can't mount the steps to church or his friends' houses or the barber shop. Can't play baseball. Can't drive. Can't work a job. Can't marry or have children. Can't do a goddamned thing he enjoyed."

"It's too soon to think like that," I said.

Henry cried silently. When he finished, he whispered, "I'm thinking about all of this misery stretching out for decades to come, for Gordy and for the whole family. I'm just going to have to accept that from now on, my life will be devoted to Gordy's needs."

Henry was beginning to see his own life limited by what Gordy couldn't do, by what Gordy needed. The martyr's life.

"I am his father, and it's my fault this all happened. I should have worked with him more before giving him his own shotgun." Henry's guilt had a friend—resentment. "It's like we were both shot today. Two lives changed forever."

I opened the door to the balcony and held it open for Henry. "I'm just going to peek in at Gordy before I head home. I can stay a while if you want me to drive you back to pick up your car." I reached into my pocket. "Here are the keys to the Fleetmaster. I meant to give them to you before."

"Thanks, but Ida isn't going anywhere tonight. She'll sleep standing up if she has to. The sister said there was a little hotel close by where we could spend the night. I'll try to get Ida to go there, but I doubt she will agree."

As we stepped back into the hospital, I noticed a clock the size of the moon hanging high on a wall. It was one of those hospital clocks where the second hand jumps from one dot to another. It was past 8:30. Henry and I had been on the balcony for almost an hour, and nobody came looking for him. Not even Ida.

II

GORDY

Deep in a morphine sleep, I existed in the purest form of life. Before awareness, before movement, and long before thought. I was left only with my original abilities: breathing and heartbeat. It was a good thing nobody needed help from me for anything. I could not give it. Riding red cells like tire tubes on a river, the chemicals that allowed me to be alive traveled through my body.

I was barely connected to the world. I could not feel the solid surface of my bed. My eyelids were as heavy as two garage doors. I did feel the hum of the machines and voices around me, but the vibrations were meaningless. And then, my senses awakened one by one. First came an antiseptic smell, then a high-pitched mechanical beep, then voices, then burning in my chest, cold liquid entering my body from the IV, the weight of eyelids opening, and finally a sliver of light.

"He's awake," a woman said. My mother. "He's back."

At first, I could not place myself. There were fences on each side of the bed. A crib? Had I returned to infancy to start my life again?

"Gordy, this is Nurse Janice. Can you hear me? Can you tell me your name?"

I opened my eyes as wide as I could. "My name is Gordon McCann."

"Very good. Your folks are here."

"Pop? Mom?"

"Right here," said Mom. "Julie is here. She's staying with Aunt Viv and Uncle Jim for now. I called Roger's mother, and she said . . ."

I could not follow Mom's rapid chatter. "I'm hungry," I said.

Mom sprang on me and hugged my neck. "Our boy is back. Thank God."

I ate some Jell-O and drank some milk. Not easy when you are flat on your back. My audience praised every swallow.

Julie skipped into the room followed by Aunt Viv. "Hi, Gordy. Sorry you got shot. I guess I'm living with Jim and Aunt Viv now," she said.

"Just for a day or two," said Pop.

"Did it hurt bad when the bullet went inside you?" Julie asked.

"Not at first."

"Do you remember me carrying you in Phil's truck?" Pop asked.

"Not really. I remember red lights. Was there an ambulance?"

"That's right," said Mom. "An ambulance brought you from Perryville." With every recollection, Mom's voice rose another octave. She leaned down close to my right ear and whispered, "We'll get that bullet out of you, and you'll be back running in no time."

A new voice spoke. "Hey, young man. You've got quite a cheering section. Mind if I have a few minutes alone with my patient?"

The family left the room in single file. They chattered down the hallway like fans of the losing team, shuffling off the bleachers to their cars.

A tall guy in a white coat looked down at me. He was wearing a big necklace (it was a stethoscope.) He had a deep but quiet voice; it sounded confident. I was relieved someone was in charge other than my family.

"I'm Dr. Dreesen. We met last night. Let's take a look at you." He pulled back the dressing under my arm and checked the wound. "Looks good," he said. He spent a lot of time looking at my legs, moving from one side of the bed to the other. Just looking.

"Can you feel that, son?"

"No. You haven't done anything."

Dr. Dreesen held up a little rubber mallet. "I've been poking you with the handle."

"Where?"

"Your legs, ankles, feet."

"Well, try it again. This medicine in my arm makes me all numb."

Dr. Dreesen removed a little instrument from his coat pocket. When he held it up, I saw it had a sharp point, like a nut pick used to harpoon the meat out of walnuts and pecans.

"Feel that?" Dr. Dreesen asked.

"No."

"How about that?"

"No."

Dr. Dreesen held the instrument up for me to see. There was a tiny drop of blood on the end. He wiped it on the sheet. "That's from your right foot," he said.

"How come I didn't feel it?" I asked.

"You have a spine injury from a gunshot wound. That's why you can't feel your legs."

I waited for more, but the doctor walked to a little sink and washed his hands.

"When will the feeling come back?" I asked when he finally turned back to face me.

"Probably never," the doctor said. He waited patiently for my next question.

"Mom says there is a bullet inside me. Are you going to take it out?"

"No," he said. He paused. I guess he thought I was going to start screaming or something. When I wouldn't give him the satisfaction, he went on. "The bullet is under a rib. It can't hurt you any further."

"Mom says if you take it out, I'll be able to walk."

"No, Gordy. One has nothing to do with the other. The bullet damaged your spine. I'm sorry. After you heal inside and the swelling goes down, we'll see about walking."

I tried to argue with the doctor. "I'm just a kid. I have to walk. I go to school and help out at home. Pop and I are building a new house. I play baseball. Not as good as my friend, Roger, but I love it. I have to run those bases."

Dr. Dreesen let me finish. When I closed my eyes, he squeezed my right hand gently. "I'm going to ask your parents to come back in now. We'll talk more later. I promise I'll answer all your questions."

"I don't want to see them," I said.

"It's your choice. Separately and together, you all have to face what's happened. You have a strong, loving family. Let them help you."

I had no more to say. What was the point? I tried to cross my arms in disgust, but the movement pulled on my IV. Now, I was angry. Madder than I ever felt in fifteen years. *What was with this guy? Was he the smartest doctor in the place? I want to talk to his boss.*

Dr. Dreesen calmly made notes on a clipboard. "Hey, Doc. I need to take a leak."

"You can feel the urge to urinate?"

"Sort of, but not like I'm used to," I said. *I was getting the royal shaft now.*

"You're wearing a catheter. A tube from your urethra into this bag on the side of your bed. It's about a quarter full. Good output."

"What bag?" I tried to push myself up on my elbows to look over the rails of the bed.

"It's down here. Don't worry, it's probably not permanent. Your wound is high enough on the thoracic part of your spine that you should regain bladder and bowel control."

"Bowel? You mean there's a tube from my ass to a bag of shit down there?" I shouted. I grabbed the rail of the bed with my free arm and shook it, like a monkey shaking the bars of his cage in a zoo.

12

PHIL

When we left Gordy's room, Julie wanted to take the stairs down to the lobby. "Want to race, Uncle Phil?" Julie asked.

"My goodness, no," I said. "You would beat me by a mile, and then I would feel so embarrassed."

Vivian touched Julie on the shoulder. "Last one down is a wet rag," she said.

I watched the ladies race down the stairs, their curly heads bobbing as they hit each step. I was glad for Julie to have a bit of fun. I was in no great hurry to rejoin Henry, the old sourpuss.

As I expected, Henry was standing in front of a chair. He was staring daggers at Viv when I opened the stairway door. His face muscles were tight, and his eyes kind of squinted. This was his impatient expression, although anyone who didn't know him would think he was very constipated.

When I reached the chairs, Julie and Viv were packing their sewing project into a canvas bag. Viv picked up a couple of books I bought her in the gift shop and handed them to Julie.

"What are you sewing there?" I asked Julie.

"It's a doll quilt. Aunt Viv is going to let me use her sewing machine when we go home. I mean, when we go to her house."

Vivian asked me if I wanted a ride back to Perryville. Henry's eyes rolled so high in his sockets I thought they might not come back down.

"No thanks. Earl is coming to get me."

"Goodbye Uncle Phil. Thanks for the ice cream." Julie gave me a nice hug around my belly. As Viv and Julie walked toward the door, Jim leaned toward my ear and said, "Hell of a thing for a father to shoot his own kid."

I did not respond. I didn't even kick him in the ass when he turned to walk away. I heard Viv tell Julie that Gordy was going to be okay and she would see him very soon.

Jim frowned at Vivian. "Now you're a doctor?" he said for all to hear.

Julie turned and faced Jim. "The doctor told me personally that Gordy would be okay, so there," she said. *That's my girl*, I thought.

"Well, then you've seen Gordy, your folks, and the treating physician. Time to go home," Jim said.

I stepped forward, but didn't slug Jim—not in front of Julie. He stood up and stretched like he had done a day's work. "Ida wants Julie to stay with us a few days," Jim said. I sensed he wanted to say, "So, there," but he was too dignified with his college degree and all. Jim made the "sigh heard 'round the world" and said, "We'll wait another half hour. It's sixty miles back to Perryville, and we both need our sleep."

Vivian took Julie's sewing and examined it. Without looking up, she said, "We will leave when Ida wants Julie to leave."

Jim smiled and shook his head in mild amusement. "I never would have believed it, but I guess it's true. After all this time being married to me, you've learned a few things. Good job, Vivie."

I3

DR. DREESEN

Gordy was a cooperative patient as he healed from his bullet wound. By the second week of his inpatient care, he was sleeping with only mild pain medication. Beginning tomorrow, Gordy would be too busy to mourn his loss. He would begin working with a physical therapist twice a day until discharge. He would have to learn transfers from bed to chair, bed to commode, and back. Gordy's teachers would visit and set up home schooling for the next few weeks. The parents needed training on turning Gordy in bed.

I planned to show Gordy his x-rays and teach him some vocabulary to talk about his spinal cord injury. He could learn to treat his paralysis as a physical condition, not a punishment. *Lots of guys enjoy baseball who can't hit a ball or run the bases for all kinds of reasons—they're too old or have lousy eyesight or just aren't coordinated enough to play sports.* Gordy would not buy that argument, of course. Not now, not when the season was just beginning. But later, even years later, he would see that what the doctor said was true. I made a mental note to talk to the parents about developing new interests—photography, woodworking, fishing, playing a musical instrument.

There would have to be a discussion of sex, now or later. The father was most likely to ask about it. I was readyafter treating dozens of paraplegic patients at the Jefferson Barracks. They had wives and girlfriends. One doctor I trained with, an old guy from the first war, brought in hookers to teach the patients some new techniques.

I worked lots of nights on the wards with injured G.I.s. It's never completely quiet in a hospital, no matter the hour. I frequently heard the sounds of men finding relief through "self-abuse." I never tried to stop them. The nurses played the phonograph at night at their desk on the ward. I called it the "V.A. Late Night Ballroom," pun intended. The nurses thought I was gross. There were only two records: Glenn Miller's *Moonlight Serenade* and Artie Shaw's *Deep Purple*.

14

GORDY

My first week in the hospital, I was never alone. Mom was there just about constantly. She stayed a couple of days at the hotel after Pop went home to get back to work. Uncle Konnie brought his family once or twice. One afternoon, Coach brought the whole baseball team to visit. After some awkward, polite talk, Coach left to get me a milkshake. The guys came up close to my bed, all except Roger Pardee. He was my best friend and not a liar. He was also a natural-born baseball player. Coach said he played like he invented the game. Off the field, Roger stayed against the walls or in the background. He was wearing that dopey hat of his with the ear flaps. Roger stood against a wall behind the other guys and let them gather around me jabbering like the goofs they were.

"Hey, Gordy, did your dad really shoot you?" Kevin Maddox asked.

"Is the bullet really still in you?" asked Calvin Simpson.

"I heard a coyote just about ripped you apart."

"Where's the baby fox you saved? Will you keep it for a pet?"

"When are you coming back to school?"

The guys were full of questions.

I told them I would likely miss the rest of the school year. That news was met with expressions of jealousy from some members of the team. Calvin voiced his opinion by saying I had it "made in the shade."

"The school is sending a teacher to help me catch up," I said.

"Oh, man! If that ain't the royal shaft. Can't play ball but you still have to do homework?"

"Shut up, Calvin," someone said.

"I wonder which teacher they'll send," Kevin said.

"Some substitute, I guess," I said.

Lyle pretended to faint dramatically. "Maybe you'll get Miss Evans. I had her last year when Mrs. Schlemmer broke her wrist. Miss Evans is stacked!"

"Yeah," the other boys agreed.

I laughed, but not convincingly.

After another nervous silence, Calvin sat in the wheelchair by my bed. At first, he rocked back and forth. Then, the shortstop grabbed the chair from behind and pushed it in a tight circle. The catcher then wanted a turn at the "wheel." He put one foot on the rear axle and tried to lift the front wheels. Then, two boys got on the chair at once. Unable to control the chair with the weird weight distribution, they crashed it into the wall. Roger jumped out of the way just in time.

"Say, Gordy, how long do you have to use this chair?" asked Lyle.

"Forever, I guess. Not this one. It belongs to the hospital. I'm getting a new one, much better. It's been ordered already."

Roger set the chair back on its wheels. The guys stepped

away from my bed and stared at the floor and the door. I said, "Where did Coach go for that milkshake? Kansas City?"

As if on cue, Coach appeared. The quiet room confused him.

"Why so quiet, guys?"

Roger stepped forward, "I think visiting hours are about over."

Coach set the milkshake on my tray. He shook my hand and turned to the boys. "Back on the bus, men. Full practice when we get back to Perryville."

The boys groaned and followed out the door, waving over their shoulders to me. Roger stayed where he was. I saw him open his mouth, but before he could speak, Calvin ran back into the room. He gasped out his question. "Can I have your bike? Pay you six bucks for it."

Roger stepped forward. Calvin had obviously forgotten he was there because he jumped back and said, "Jesus H. Christ."

"What makes you think his bike is for sale?" Roger asked.

"Because, I mean, you need legs to ride a bike," Calvin said.

"He has legs. Two of them. One to kick your ass and one to spare," said Roger.

Calvin faced Roger. This was between them. I was just watching from the Peanut Gallery. Calvin covered one side of his mouth and said in a low voice through clenched teeth, "You know Coach said Gordy's never going to walk again," he said.

"So, Coach is a doctor, now?" Roger said.

"No. I'm trying to do the guy a favor. Teammate to team-mate, you know? If it turns out—and I hope it doesn't—that he can't walk again, I'm offering him some cash for something he can't use anyway."

"A favor? That's what this is?" asked Roger.

"Sure," said Calvin. He acted like he had slid into first base on a bunt.

"Six bucks isn't much of a favor," Roger said. He looked

over his shoulder at me, giving Calvin a personal, illuminated view of the left side of his head. The skin over Roger's ear—what was left of his ear—was pulled tight. Beneath the white scars covering his scalp like a messy paint job, his skin glowed pink in the fluorescent light. Roger was showing that he was not afraid of whatever trouble or pain Calvin thought he could deal. This was Roger, the boy who ran into a fire to save his mother. He didn't have to prove a thing.

"How much then?" asked Calvin.

"How much?" Roger tossed the question to me.

"More than you'll ever have," I said. Double play. Game over.

Calvin ran out of the room. Roger tugged his ridiculous hat down over his orange curls. "Gotta get on the bus," he said as he walked out of the door into the puke green tile hall.

Once, on the way to a game, I heard one of the coaches say that Roger played like he was born in a dugout. If he ever missed a pop fly or a grounder, I don't remember it. Coach had to tell him to quit wasting energy running after foul pop-ups. "Let them go. Save your energy for a solid hit."

Roger shrugged and said, "You want me to throw away an easy out?"

"Easy? Never. Smashing your body against the fence or running up the bleachers is an unnecessary risk of injury."

"I'm not scared," Roger said.

"Son, no one better say you aren't brave within my hearing."

For the rest of the evening, I tried to think of all the things I had not lost at Cinque Hommes Creek. It was not a very long list, but there was room to grow.

15

DR. DREESEN

Parents are full of questions about spinal cord injuries. Some tell me about a person they knew or heard about who was seriously injured but learned to not only walk again but became a bank president or something. Mrs. McCann was no exception. She sat as close as she could to the bed when I examined Gordy. Mr. McCann stood by the window during examinations. He was holding on to the world outside the window. He was suffering double—for Gordy's disability and for his assumed guilt for causing it. At the end of the exam, I said, "He's making good progress. Exactly what we hoped to see." It was vague but true.

"Would you like to talk more in my office?" I asked.

She turned to Gordy and said, "We'll be back in a few minutes."

I waited in the hall for Mrs. McCann to come out of the room. Henry followed her, watching his feet as he walked. He looked like he was studying the process: lift the right heel a second after the left heel touches the floor ahead of the right. The feet are propelled from the hips into a rolling motion. The sequence of actions is quite complex. Maybe Henry remembered Gordy's first wobbly steps.

Six shoes in motion made for quite a racket on the marble floor. The 20-foot ceilings converted the old halls into a powerful echo chamber. Old hospitals were built like cathedrals; lots of stone and high carved ceilings. St. Anthony's opened in 1900, long before medical centers became boxy complexes housing huge treatment machines, laboratories, and single-patient rooms with bathrooms equipped for any accommodation needed. Healing changed from a partnership with faith to a worship of science.

I brought the McCanns into my office. "Come in, please. How are you both doing? Did you get any sleep last night?"

"Hardly any," Mrs. McCann said.

Henry walked past the two chairs in front of my desk and walked to the window. I emptied both chairs of files and journals so they could sit.

Henry took the chair next to his wife. She began with a question I had not expected. "What about President Roosevelt?"

"His paralysis was caused by a virus," I said.

"Yes, but he learned to walk again."

"He had lots of help: people holding him up, railings he could pull himself along with, special braces. The President never walked very far. Just a few steps for the cameras."

"Well, he didn't have to use a wheelchair," she said.

"Of course, he did," said Henry. He shifted in his seat to face his wife. "Roosevelt didn't allow pictures of it. A president can hide anything he wants."

Mrs. McCann said, "I read that the President swam to strengthen his legs."

"Swimming is good exercise for the cardiovascular system," I agreed. "But Gordy's paralysis is different from the President's. The polio virus causes inflammation of muscles that cause them to weaken. Gordy has what we call an incomplete spinal cord injury. The injury to his spinal cord interrupts nerve impulses from his brain to his legs."

"The result is the same, though," she said.

"Very similar."

"Could you remove the damaged part of his spinal cord and sew the two ends back together?" she asked. Poor lady was really grasping at straws.

"No. Gordy's spinal cord is not severed. If a spinal cord is severed, death usually results.

Gordy's thoracic spinal cord was banged around inside the thoracic vertebrae when the projectile passed through his body and made waves. The cord was bruised and some of the nerve paths were damaged. His wound will heal, but at this time we cannot regenerate nerves."

"Will his legs grow any more or stay the size they are now?"

"What about crutches?"

Mr. McCann asked, "Is there research going on that might help Gordy to walk again? Maybe we should take him somewhere like the Mayo Clinic. What do you think about that?"

"Let's not get ahead of ourselves. Research is in very early stages," I said.

Mrs. McCann asked a mother's question. "Will his legs get skinny?"

"In time. We'll do physical therapy here to prevent loss of circulation and muscle tone as much as possible."

"And when he goes home?"

"We'll teach you and your husband what to do when the time comes."

I rose and picked up a file from my desk. "I have to see another patient. I have Gordy scheduled to start working with a physical therapist tomorrow. Nothing strenuous, of course. He just had surgery. Just some easy movements for now. Let's talk again tomorrow afternoon."

16

GORDY

At the end of my first week at St. Anthony's Gimpville, Clayton Pinchon knocked on my door and entered before I could answer. "Morning, Glory. Ready for some dancing in place?" Clayton crowed.

"Sure. Come on in," I said.

"I'll be your physical therapist."

"Okay. What do I call you?"

"Well, my name is Clayton. May I call you Gordon?"

"That's my name, don't wear it out," I said.

Clayton laughed like he had never heard that before. He was a little guy, not much taller than Julie. Skinny but muscular, not bulky like a bodybuilder. He had dark skin and big hands. He was a miniature Bill Russell, but he talked like Mickey Rooney.

Clayton connected a kind of trapeze to the overhead frame of my bed. He then lowered the head of the bed a few inches with the crank at the foot. Was he intentionally making it harder for me? "I want maximum effort today. Pull yourself up.

Slowly, slowly. We build more muscle going slowly," Clayton said.

I grabbed for the bar and missed the first couple of tries. Clayton put his hand on my back. "Just hang on for a minute. Let your muscles get used to the position."

When I was ready, I pulled myself into a half-sitting position. My arms trembled with the effort, but I did not let go.

"Nicely done. Let's try four pull-ups today. No! You know what? Why don't you show me how many pull-ups you can do? Keep your neck straight. Don't let it hang to the back. No hunching the shoulders. Good for the arms and the abdomen."

I did nine pull-ups that day. Well, five good ones. Clayton was strong but patient. He let me try as hard as I could, but he knew when to step in. It was pretty obvious that Clayton was a different kind of guy. If Kevin Maddox or one of the other guys saw him, they would be giggling the rest of the day and whispering "fag" or "queer" whenever their laughter died down. I didn't think about it too much. When he was with me, we worked hard.

One day, after a morning session, Clayton asked if he could bring his lunch and we could eat together. I hesitated. "Isn't that against the rules? Fraternizing with patients?"

"Not at all."

At lunchtime, Clayton pulled up a chair and shared the bed table with me.

"How did you get into this physical therapy racket?" I asked.

"I grew up in Chicago. I was a mess as a kid: I ate too much and got fat. My mother would say, 'Clayton, you ain't fat. Your muscles are just a little bit lazy about holding you all in.'

"Once I saw a ballet performance. I snuck into the theatre

to escape some rough kids who liked to chase me. Not important. Anyway, I watched two dancers rehearsing. A man and a
woman. The woman fell asleep in a chair and then woke up
and danced with the man, like in a dream. The male dancer's
leg muscles were enormous. Every muscle was visible through
his tights. At the end, the male dancer jumped through an
open window. He just lifted himself off the ground and flew.
He had more than strength, though. He owned his body."

"So, you studied ballet dancing?"

"I considered it. But if I had asked my father to pay for
ballet lessons, he would have thrown me through a window. I
took up boxing. I hated fighting but I loved the training. It
made me the man I am today."

After a week of twice-daily therapy sessions, my family came
for a visit. Clayton and I were about to start working. He introduced himself and asked them to stay and watch the action. He
pinched my bicep and said, "Check out those muscles. After
only eight sessions."

I thought Pop was going to flip. I don't know if he was
more flabbergasted by my new little bicep muscles or by
Clayton.

Clayton was a good teacher. He demonstrated how to bend
my knees toward my chest, one at a time. "Slowly, always
slowly."

I lifted hand weights while sitting in a straight chair. I was
tied to the back of the chair to prevent me from losing balance
and falling. Again, Mom gasped when she watched me strap
myself in.

Clayton talked me through. "Chin up. Straight arms. Lock
the elbows. Hold, hold, hold, and slowly down. Sir, your boy is
a champ."

The family sat down and watched my work begin. "Now, Gordon will be able to lift his legs on his own before he leaves the hospital, but he'll need help. We use a little trick to accomplish that: a folded towel. That's where he'll need some help at first, positioning the towel. Where did I put that? For heaven's sake, I forgot the towel. Let me grab one from the nurse's station."

"What about this?" Julie said. She had her jump rope tied around her waist. She handed it to Clayton.

"Out of the mouths of babes. Thanks, sweetie."

Mom stared daggers at Julie. "I told you to leave that in the car."

Clayton tested the rope's strength. "Now, Julie may have come up with something great here. When we patent it, we'll call it the Julie Stretcher."

Clayton doubled the jump rope and placed it in the arch of my left foot. Satisfied that the rope might work, I transferred myself back to the bed.

"Hey there, Gordon, bet you didn't expect to be using one of these any time soon."

"Just stand back and watch me," I said. This seemed like a very important moment. Whatever I was to become depended on my performance right here, right now. "Watch and learn, Julie," I said.

My foot looked like it was a mile away down there at the end of the bed. I laid down the ends of the rope and pulled myself up to a sitting position with the bar overhead. That was the easy part. If I let go of the bar, I might fall backwards, but I needed two hands to fling the rope around my foot.

"Help him," Mom said to Clayton.

"Do you want help, Gordon?" Clayton asked.

"Everybody just cool it a minute."

I grasped the bar and studied the terrain of my lower body. I pulled myself up a little more and slung my left arm over the bar, catching it in the crook of my elbow. This caused me to tip, but I scooted back into position. Holding the wooden handles of the jump rope in my right hand, I flung the doubled rope over my right foot. Of course, I missed by a mile. On the next try, I dropped one of the rope handles. It landed on my knee. Everyone in the room started to step forward to retrieve the end of the rope.

"Give me a chance. I can get it," I yelled.

I gathered the rope up with my left hand, passed the handle to my right, and tossed the rope. This time it landed beyond my foot. Now, all I had to do was control the rope with both handles in one hand and slowly pull the loop around the bottom of my foot. It would be easier if the right foot was up straight pointing to the ceiling instead of listing to the side as it did. I tried to move my right foot. Of course, that didn't work.

"There has to be a better piece of equipment for this than a dime-store jump rope," Pop said. Mom shushed him, but Pop continued. "I'm serious. In this world-famous hospital, known for its work with paralyzed patients, you're telling me that a rolled-up towel and a jump rope are the best devices you have to help my son?"

"They are the most readily available. Gordon's learning to improvise. He will be improvising many things for many years. Go on, Gordon. What's your next move?"

I was still hanging by my left arm from the bar. I considered trying to throw the rope again for a better position, but my left arm was already trembling from the exertion.

I dropped one of the jump-rope handles onto my thigh. Then, I let go of the bar, and as I fell back onto the pillow, I grabbed at the rope handle with my left hand. Now, I had a handle in each hand, although I was on my back again. By pulling one way and then another with the handles of the rope, I managed to get the center of the rope under the arch of my right foot.

I began to pull slowly upward on the rope. My foot was no help at all, and the movement of the rope caused the foot to flex, and the rope came up over my toes and laid limp on my shin.

"Shit!" I cried.

I began again, using the bar. After a short lifetime, I got the rope back into position under my foot. I let go of the bar and jerked on the rope as I fell backward. The jump rope didn't have a chance to roll out of position. I pulled slowly on the two ends of the rope, and my right foot rose from the dead. My family applauded, but I realized I could not bend my knee by myself.

I gave the rope some slack and worked it under the heel of the foot. Then, I drew the rope up under my right knee,and the knee began to bend. The bottom part of my leg dragged on the bed. I hadn't expected that, but I kept pulling slowly as my knee rose toward my chin and my foot and calf hung loose beneath it. I continued slowly pulling my knee toward my chest, wrapping the excess rope around my wrists as I went.

"Give that boy a lollipop!" Clayton said. I felt as if I had rung the bell on the strong-man game at a carnival.

"Now, let's see you lower the leg," Clayton whispered. "Let gravity be your friend."

I slackened the rope to let my knee drop. When it dropped, my right heel hit the bed, blocking the leg from straightening itself. Gravity was trying to pull the leg down, but it was caught.

My brain searched its archive of leg-lowering commands. I believed I was lifting my foot. I was doing everything right, but when I looked down, the foot had not moved at all. It was not getting the message from my brain.

Clayton told me to relax and try again. I closed my eyes and pictured my leg straightening out on the bed. I could see it so clearly that I was sure the leg must have lowered a few inches at least. I opened my eyes. Nothing.

"Goddamn it. Stupid leg. Shit, shit, shit."

Mom clasped her hands together under her chin. Probably praying for God to forgive my blasphemy and reminding Him that He could be helping more.

I had an idea. I pulled the rope so that my knee moved slightly to the right. This eased the tension on my heel, and my foot started sliding right down. Like water running downhill, the foot slid toward the end of the bed, and my leg lowered. In the end, both legs were on the bed—not exactly parallel—but good enough for Clayton to clap his hands.

I smiled. "One," I said.

Everyone laughed. My journey back had begun.

"Gordon has done so well building his upper body strength, we can start working on transfers to the wheelchair soon." Clayton turned to me and continued, "You'll be able to ditch the bedpan, buddy. We'll celebrate that, won't we?"

Clayton brought the wheelchair close to the bed. "While he's been healing and gaining strength, Gordon has needed help with his transfers. He will need to learn to do those by himself: from bed to chair, chair to car, and also how to go up and down curbs. When he masters all of that—and I know he will in record time—he will be more independently mobile."

Pop examined the chair from top to bottom. I prayed he would not kick the tires.

"What's the lifespan of one of these contraptions?" he asked.

"Years and years. The tires wear out and the seat gets worn, but parts are replaceable."

"Do they make racing wheelchairs?" I asked.

"Good question," Clayton said. "Not yet, but maybe you and I could come up with one. Make our fortune."

I shook Clayton's hand. "Deal."

Clayton turned to my parents. "We've got ourselves a wheel man here." Only Julie laughed.

17

GORDY

"Good morning, sunshine," Clayton had arrived with his usual version of sweet annoyance.

"Welcome to your first day driving a wheelchair. There is no written test, no manual, and no learner's permit. This is your mobility for a lifetime, boys and girls, so get it right. Remember: practice makes perfect, and gravity is a law."

There it was. A chair with wheels, or as we in the business call it: a wheelchair. My new friend for life.

Lesson one was transferring from the hospital bed to the chair.

Attempt Number One: Although you might think that grabbing the trapeze bar over my bed, then swinging myself to a position directly on top of the chair, and then letting go of the bar would be a good idea, it is not. First, the bar does swivel, but it does not swing. It is suspended by a chain that does not stretch. At all. Even if the chair is right up against the bed, you cannot swing your body laterally far enough to position your body directly over the chair. If you miss the center of the seat, even by a little, you topple the chair and fall on the floor. Ouch.

Attempt Number Two: Scoot to the side of the bed and drop the legs over the side in a normal sitting position. Bring the chair close to the bed. With one hand on the seat of the chair and the other hand on the bed, lift your body and swing laterally until you are in the chair, and then scoot your ass to get into a straight sitting position and lift your feet onto the footrests. Be sure to make your hands into fists before pushing off the bed. Using a flat hand is murder on the wrist. Also, be sure the brakes are set on the chair or else the chair will roll, your body will be suspended between bed and chair, and eventually, you will fall to the floor. Ouch.

Once in the chair, ready to zoom off to the bathroom, dining room, or anywhere you want to go, just push the wheels forward with both hands. Or so I thought.

It might seem a good conservation of energy to push forward on the wheels with all your strength and coast at top speed. However, few people have absolutely equal strength in both their arms, so you will likely not take off in a straight line. Remember, too, that when you are inside a building, you have to deal with annoying walls, forcing you to turn. Rolling at top speed (about 3 mph), it is difficult to slow the chair enough to make a right-angle turn. You will burn the skin off the palms of your hands, at the very least. At worst, you will crash into a wall and be thrown onto the floor. Again. Ouch.

A steady, moderate pace is always the safest. True, you won't feel the wind in your hair, but you will not crack your head against a wall or floor. I have proven this.

Let's say you want to leave a room and need to close the door behind you. For this, you need a rope or strap. Even an umbrella will do for hooking the door knob as you roll through the doorway. No need to remove the rope, belt, or umbrella; just leave it hanging on the door. An old necktie works equally well, and since you aren't going to any formal dances any time soon, why not? Another useful device is your sister's favorite headscarf. The downside seems obvious. Ouch.

The time will come, believe me, when you need to turn your wheelchair. Again, a lower speed is not only advisable but necessary. In order to turn on a curve or at a sharp angle, you need to roll the wheel backward on the side where you want to turn. Roll the opposite wheel forward to make the turn. In this maneuver, gravity is not your friend. Slow down, Speedy Gonzalez. Leave the rubber burning to the pros.

Tune in again when I will elaborate on the cruelest invention of all—stairs.

18

DR. DREESEN

"Any idea when I might be going home?" Gordy asked.

"Don't you like our hospitality?"

"It's not that. I've been looking out this one window for weeks now. I know every leaf on every tree and all the birds by name."

"Why don't you wheel yourself outside?" I suggested. "Get a change of scenery. How are your transfers to the chair?"

"Piece of cake," he said. The idea of independent mobility in the outside world put a smile on his face. "Rolling around these smooth floors is kid's stuff."

"Show me," I said.

Gordy threw back the sheet covering his legs. He reached up for the bar overhead. Before he could grab it, he was knocked back onto the bed. Gordy's legs twitched and contorted. The spasms were so strong they pulled his pelvis, which pulled his upper body. He looked in horror at his spastic legs and feet.

"Hell's bells! What's happening?" he screamed.

Without thinking, I said, "I didn't expect it this soon." I reached for Gordy's chart to make notes.

"This is ... normal?" Gordy growled.

"Unfortunately, yes."

"When does it stop?"

"It depends on the location of the spinal cord injury. I'm afraid the thoracic spine is one of those sites."

"So, you can't do anything to stop this rabbit kicking?" he begged.

"It's a common sequela in children with spinal cord injuries. That just means a condition caused by an injury. We should be able to at least reduce it. I'll call your physical therapist, get him to see you three times a day. Stretching helps,and range of motion exercises will help reduce the muscle tightness. Hot packs can help. I'll let the nurse know."

"If it's stretching you want, I'll do it all day long," Gordy said.

"That's the spirit. I'm afraid the only way to stop the spasms entirely is by selective dorsal rhizotomy. It's surgery."

"I guess if you have to knock me out again, let's get to it," he said.

"I'll need to talk to your parents. Have the nurse page me when they come in. If I'm not in the hospital, we can talk by phone."

19

GORDY

It was late afternoon when Mom and Pop arrived. It was a workday for Pop. Uncle Jim picked up Julie from school. I pulled up a blanket to cover my legs. It didn't work. They noticed my legs jerking right away. Mom nearly had a cow. "Henry, look. He can move his legs. Come see. He's moving his legs. Show your dad," she said.

"Does the doc know about this?" Pop asked.

"Yeah, he saw it this morning."

Mom ran out of my room. I heard her shoes marching down the hall, then her hand hitting the nurses' counter, and her piercing demand that Dr. Dreesen be called at once.

The doc came on the double. He probably heard Mom all the way down the hall from his office. When he came into the room, Mom pointed to my legs and put her fists on her hips. This posture meant she was very serious. "See, he's moving his legs. He's getting better. He'll be cured. Oh, baby, I've been praying so hard."

"I'm not moving them, Mom. The muscles are moving on their own. I have no control."

Mom looked at Pop, but he had nothing to say. "What can be done?" she asked the doc.

Dr. Dreesen did not answer immediately. He asked Mom and Pop to sit down first. He explained how spastic diplegia can set in after a spinal cord injury.

"It's very common in patients with traumatic spinal cord injuries. Also, children with cerebral palsy can have this symptom. At first, the paralysis in Gordy's legs was flaccid. The legs were limp because of the trauma to the spinal cord. His legs were not getting messages from his spinal cord to flex and move as they normally do. As the spinal cord heals, the nerves coming out of it trigger involuntary reflex activity. Gordy's neurons are firing without instruction, without purpose. It's uncomfortable for him and hinders his mobility."

"Do the spasms stop after a while?" Pop asked.

"Unfortunately, no. We can only stop them surgically. It will help Gordy's overall condition. Patients with these spasms have difficulty sleeping. The surgery also often helps patients with their bladder function."

I interrupted the doc. "Can you do it today?"

"That's a decision you and your folks will have to make."

Mom started to cry. Pop moved his chair closer to her and held her hand. "Tell us more about the surgery."

"The procedure is called a selective dorsal rhizotomy. It has been performed on thousands of kids with cerebral palsy and worldwide on traumatic SCI patients. We can assess which nerve rootlets are causing the muscle contraction. Then, we go in the back through a very small incision and destroy the nerve rootlets causing the spasticity."

"And how would you 'destroy' these disobedient nerve roots?" Pop asked.

"By cutting them."

"If the nerves are cut, they can't heal. Not even in the future when doctors know more than we do now," Mom said.

"That's correct. Nerves that are severed don't regenerate," said the doc.

Pop looked at me. "We'll have to talk about this some more. Gordy should have a say in what happens to him."

I pulled myself up with the bar. "Mom, I can't live like this. I look like Julie's wind-up monkey. All I need are a pair of cymbals and a tin cup for people to drop in their nickels. Which street should I sit on? Would I get more sympathy closer to the grocery store? The ESSO station? Oh wait, a church. But which one? Which church do you think is more generous, Mom?"

"Stop it, Gordy," Pop said. "Your mother and I weren't expecting this, that's all. Give us some credit for wanting to make a good decision."

"How much longer will Gordy have to stay in the hospital?" Mom asked.

"A couple of weeks. We'll take good care of him," said the doc.

No one spoke. Invisible bolts of anger and fear erupted throughout the room. As they began to settle, to sporadically sizzle, Mom leaned forward in her chair. "When can you do the operation?" she asked quietly. The effort to control her voice was visible in her face.

"I'll check the schedule. Tomorrow most likely," Dr. Dreesen answered.

"We'll be here," said Pop. Mom released Pop's hand.

Without taking her eyes off me, Mom said to Dr. Dreesen, "Proceed, then. While you are inside my son's body, if you would be so kind, remove the bullet, please."

"I won't be anywhere near it," the doc said. He hesitated a

moment, reluctant to leave with Mom still so upset. "Mr. McCann, your vote?"

"Do whatever you can," he said.

Dr. Dreesen left, saying he needed to reserve an O.R. right away or lose a spot on the next day's schedule.

Mom reached for her handbag. "I'll call Viv and see if Julie can stay with her tonight. If you want to get a hotel room, Henry, go right ahead. I'll be perfectly comfortable right here for the night."

"Ida, honey, please. Gordy will rest better if he knows you are comfortable. You call Viv and I'll find a hotel room." Pop did not wait for a response but left the room, digging in his pocket for change for the telephone.

"Gordy, I wouldn't leave you for the world unless you are sure you're not too scared," she said.

"I'm plenty scared, but also tired. Clayton is worse than Uncle Jim when he's coaching Little League."

Mom smiled. "He hates coaching Little League. He hates kids, but you didn't hear that from me."

"I think every student he ever taught or coached knows that."

"Gordy, I didn't expect to have to start giving you up nearly this soon—and never to something so cruel and painful for you. I think you're getting stronger already. Is there anything you want before I go?"

"Would you massage my legs a minute? The spasms have stopped for now."

Mom kneaded my thighs and calves. Since Clayton told her that massage was good for my circulation, she had been kneading me like bread dough. We both liked it.

"Do you need anything else?"

"One more thing: make up with Pop," I said.

"We'll be fine, sweetheart. We both love you. We just have to get used to this new life, is all."

"Don't be mad at Dr. Dreesen, either. He's a good guy. Oh, and don't be mad at Uncle Phil."

"You're not leaving me very many choices here," Mom smiled.

"You can still be mad at Uncle Jim."

"Always," Mom said. "Now, where's my change purse? The phones in this hospital cost fifteen cents for a toll call. You'd think a hospital would at least give the patients and their families a break."

Satisfied that Mom's indignation against Bell Telephone would see her through the night, I switched off the light over my bed and watched the waning moon rise. I liked lying in the moonlight for some reason. I remembered a story from first or second grade about a huge snake that was in love with the moon. He climbed a high hill and talked to her at night. Once they talked so long that the moon was still in the sky when the sun came up. The sun got mad and chopped the snake into little pieces, and that's why there are no big snakes today. *Maybe I should write a coyote story*, I thought. *How the boy saved a fox kit and the stalking coyote chased him.* I didn't have an ending for the story yet. Pretty soon, I fell asleep.

When they brought me back to my room after the surgery to stop my leg spasms, Mom was there. She pulled a chair up to my bed and touched my legs very gently. I was only half-asleep. A nurse came in to check my vitals. She brought Mom a plate with a sliced apple and some cheese.

"Our lives have definitely changed," Mom said.

"Gordy is young and strong. I can see he has a supportive family. He's lucky in that respect."

"I remember having this same fear when Gordy was born. When they brought him in to me, he was so beautiful. I thought, 'I did well, brought forth a healthy baby boy.' Of course, he was all cleaned up and wrapped in a warm blanket. 'He's all yours now,' they said.

"At first, I thought I could never be responsible for such a fragile little thing. The realization of my responsibility nearly crushed my maternal confidence. You know what the nurse said? She said, 'Every new mother feels frightened. Just follow your instincts, give him lots of love, and don't believe everything people tell you. You'll both be fine.'"

After the nurse finished checking me and I was alone with Mom, I opened my eyes. She looked at me so intensely, like she was putting a spell on me or willing me to be well.

"You're awake," she said. "How do you feel?"

I didn't really know. I was still pretty groggy. "Are my legs dancing?" I asked.

"Not a bit," Mom said. "You know, Gordy, I never took care of a person in a wheelchair before. I have a lot to learn. I hope you'll be patient with me."

I wasn't the son she woke up to on the morning of April 23, 1955. He was gone. Once I figured out who I was since that fateful day, I could introduce the new Gordy to her and the rest of my family. It happened to me, so I had to take the lead with this new life thing. The Wheel Man had arrived, and he was one bad badass hipster. Dig?

20

PHIL

Ida's sister Eileen volunteered—no, she insisted—on meeting the truck delivering the trapeze bar and commode to the house for Gordy. I was there helping the concrete men pour an addition to the foundation on the new house. Konnie pulled his station wagon into the driveway of Henry's old house. I met them in the driveway. Konnie complimented me on the work thus far. Eileen said, "So, it's back to square one then?"

"No one sees the future, darling," Konnie said.

Eileen pulled a large string bag out of the car behind her. She had brought lunch for the boys and cleaning supplies to occupy herself during the wait. Cleaning was not a job to Eileen. Jobs could be completed; cleaning was eternal. With Ida's frequent absences to visit Gordy in St. Louis, Eileen was certain to find some dusty corner or dirty dish to clean.

Landis and Jefferson saw a fort in the stacks of lumber beside the foundation. They began climbing in and out of the openings in the trusses. The concrete slab became, for them, a frozen river, molten volcanic flow, or the surface of an alien planet where the inhabitants were both invisible and deadly. They looked sad when they heard their parents talking about Gordy, but between conversations, their lives continued. Not even Gordy would begrudge them the adventures waiting for them in the remains of what the family had already started referring to as "Gordy's house."

Eileen called after the twins, "Boys, when the delivery truck comes, you point it toward the old house and stay out of the way. Stay close and don't get dirty." She knew the boys were unlikely to heed her words, but she felt duty-bound to instruct them.

Inside Ida's house, I helped Konnie move the dining room table closer to the big window. We carried Gordy's bed down from his bedroom on the second floor. In the corner of the dining room, against the wall opposite the three windows, was the best place for Gordy's bed. The only place, really. Ida's walnut hutch, filled with dishes, linens, and photo albums, occupied the space where we were planning to put the bed, so it had to be unloaded and moved as well. I went into a closet behind the living room and started measuring. This would become Gordy's bathroom until the new house was finished. There was room for a toilet and a sink. It was too small for a shower you could stand in. Konnie was working on a unique design so Gordy could sit in the shower. Until it was built, he could wash in the sink. They call it a "whore's bath." I decided not to tell Gordy that particular fact.

"Landis, Jefferson. Come help," Konnie called. The boys took at least five minutes to complete their play and walk across the yard between the houses. Finally, the family formed a dish brigade across the dining room. Konnie removed a plate from the hutch, handed it to Jefferson ("Two hands, boys"), who handed it off to Landis, who placed the plate in his mother's waiting hands. She stacked the dishes on the table. When Konnie handed a bowl or cup to Landis, he said, "Thank you." Landis started saying "Thank you" to Jefferson at the hand-off. Soon the boys were shouting "THANK YOU" at the top of their voices. The sound echoed in the emptied dining room. Konnie began to say, "*Danke*." Finally, Eileen joined in by singing a contralto chorus of *Come, Ye Thankful People Come*. When it came time to reload the relocated hutch, Eileen shooed the boys outside. She told Konnie they were raising two wild monkeys. He agreed but offered no remedy.

When Gordy's bed and other equipment were in place, Eileen looked at the corner and folded her arms.

"What is it, darling?" Konnie said.

"That boy has no privacy," she said.

Konnie pulled a small notebook from his shirt pocket. He had been thinking the same thing. "Here is what I propose," he said. He quickly sketched a long dowel suspended by short chains from the ceiling. "We hang a big curtain that Gordy can pull to block the rest of the room."

"Excellent. Give me the car keys. I'll go into town and see what I can find for the drape. It has to be heavy to block sound. I'll pick up Vivian. She knows more about fabric than I do."

"What about me?" Konnie asked.

"You get the chains installed."

"What about the boys?" Konnie raised his eyebrows in an expression of exaggerated fear.

"I guess use some chain on them," Eileen said over her shoulder on her way out the door.

Off she drove in a bluster of spinning tires and flying gravel. I helped Konnie pick through Henry's lumber pile for a piece to use on the ceiling to support the weight of the huge curtain. He would drill through the ceiling into the floor joists of the second floor. Eileen had driven off so quickly that he had no time to retrieve his drill from the station wagon. Konnie clipped the tin ribbon on a stack of two-by-fours and selected one from the middle. He left the boys with strict instructions not to move any of the lumber to build a rocket ship. Konnie entered Henry's garage for a drill and some four-inch screws, if he had any. Konnie knew the boys would immediately invade the woodpile and leave him to work in peace.

21

DR. DREESEN

After Gordon's rhizotomy procedure, his leg spasms stopped. He spent the next few days resting and working with Clayton. I got busy with reports in my office. Not my favorite part of the practice of medicine, but indispensable. Sister Alison offered to straighten my office every week or so, but I did not let her. I told her my office reflected my specialty: the tangle of nerves coming from the spinal cord. "It looks chaotic, but the nerves know where they are going." Once I put down a file in my office, on the desk, chair, windowsill, bookcase, or on top of my desk lamp, its location was locked into my brain. If someone moved a file, it was as good as lost. Sister Alison said I was just making excuses. She was right.

Jean Beaumont knocked on the office door. She stood outside until I said, "Come in." Most hospital staff knocked and entered immediately. Some forewent the knock completely. Jean was neither a doctor, staff, patient, nor family member, so she waited.

"Hi, Doc. Are you busy?"

"Swamped up to my frontal lobe, but I've got a few minutes for a good friend."

I treated Jean's father when she was about six. He had a complicated leg amputation as a result of a war injury when I was at Jefferson Barracks.

At age six, Jean wore a mass of tangled, copper curls. Apparently, her mother did not brush her hair, and the curls became so matted that pulling a brush or comb through the mess was too painful for Jean. One of the nurses worked with her, cutting what could not be untangled. Jean was so skinny as a little girl that her dresses did not touch her body below the collar.

Now, here she was, in high school. Neat, shiny auburn curls flecked with copper framed her round face. My door was always open to Jean.

Jean sat in one of the chairs facing my desk. She sat down carefully, afraid that any noise or movement might upset the tower of files and books on the desk.

"How did you get here?" I asked.

"Bus. Well, two buses. I spent hours studying the bus routes. I had to transfer twice, but here I am."

"I'm glad to see you. So, what's so important you couldn't have called me?"

"Oh, I could have called. I just needed to get away."

"Shall we take a break in the cafeteria?" If Jean needed to see me this urgently, something important was on her mind. I wanted to give her time, in comfortable surroundings, to tell me about it.

"No thanks. I don't want to interrupt your work. Go ahead and see your patients. I'll stay here and put away some of these files for you," Jean said. She scooted to the edge of her seat, ready to rise and start filing as soon as I gave the word.

I shook my head. "There is confidential information in

those files. Besides, there is no money in the budget to pay for a file clerk. I already asked."

"You wouldn't have to pay me," Jean said as she settled back in the chair. Her voice was quiet, her shoulders hunched forward. She was about to speak from a painful place.

I crossed my right leg over the left. Jean saw that I was wearing no shoes and my socks were bright yellow. She didn't tease me about the socks or smile.

Jean was a delicate little girl, but she was tough. She did not call me very often for help. I told myself it meant she was doing fine. What I should have done was call her, asked her how things were going in her life. Isn't that what friends who are not doctors do?

"What did you need to get away from? School or the foster home?" I asked.

"Yes and yes."

"What's the problem?"

"No problem. Just, well, school's nearly out. I cinched my grades. I mean, they can't fail me at this late date, not unless I got in a fight or set the home ec room on fire. Can they?"

"Which one did you do?"

"A little of both?"

"Details, please."

Jean heaved the adolescent sigh of confession and began. "A girl in my home ec class said I had no sense of style. About the only clothes I have are what previous foster kids left behind, and so, I wear my favorite two dresses all the time. I alternate them. And I try to jazz them up a little, with necklaces or belts my foster mom loans me."

"You look nice today."

"Thanks. This dress came from, well, never mind that."

"So, you decked the girl who criticized your wardrobe?" I asked.

"In a way."

"Unacceptable, Jean. You look fine to me."

"I'm okay for now, I guess."

"Solved. What about the fire?"

"Well, when this high fashion *la-de-da* ran off, she left a sweater behind. Pink with pearl buttons. I just wanted to hide it for a while. I was going to give it back."

"You hid it in an oven, I'm guessing," I said. I tried to keep a stern countenance, but I so wanted to smile.

Jean leaned forward as if addressing a judge.

"How could I know the next class was making French toast in the oven? You gotta preheat the thing to 375°. Did you know that?"

"I did not." I was eager for the punchline.

"Who turns on a stove without opening the door first to check inside? Maybe a cat crawled in or something. Anyway, cotton must not take heat very well. When one of the ninth graders opened the oven door to put in her egg-soaked bread, the pink sweater was sort of on fire."

"That's how the home ec room burned?"

"The whole room didn't burn. When the ninth grader opened the oven door, she jumped back and dropped the pan with the French toast. The oven mitt on her hand fell into the oven and caught fire. It fell out of the oven onto the floor and melted the linoleum. Stunk pretty bad, I'm told."

"What about the pink sweater?"

"That's more or less why I am here. I have to replace it. I don't have any money. I can't ask my foster mom. She's stretched thin as it is."

"So, you came all the way to St. Anthony's to put the bite on me?"

"Early birthday present?"

I rose and pulled out a file from near the top of the stack. "I've got patients to see. If you can sit nicely out in the waiting room without cold-cocking any of the staff or burning anything, I'll take you shopping when I finish. This time only. Call your foster mom and tell her where you are. I'll drive you home."

There were about twelve things wrong with this plan, but I shrugged them off mentally. I stood over her while she made her phone call, in case the foster mother would ask for corroboration of Jean's story. If she didn't, then she had not been in the foster system long enough.

When the call was completed, we walked out of the office. I pointed to a row of chairs in the hall. Jean made a step toward them. "On second thought, come with me," I said.

I heard two sets of footsteps heading down the hall to my room. A young female voice said, "What an ugly shade of green." Then I heard Dr. Dreesen laugh. The halls were great echo chambers. I wondered what Tony Bennett or Elvis might sound like belting one out in them. I was sitting in my chair at the little table in my room, my back to the door. I didn't turn around at first. I heard the doc say to someone, "It's all right. Come on in." Then he said to me, "Gordy, I want you to meet someone."

So, now I'm the patient on display, I thought. It was fine. I was doing math homework. Any excuse to put algebra aside was cool with me. When I turned my chair to face the door, a petite girl with copper curls was standing there. "Hello," she said with a shy little wave.

"Come in, please," I said. "The room is kind of a mess."

Dr. Dreesen took over the introductions. "This is Jean Beaumont. She's a friend, and I thought maybe you could keep each other company while I finish my rounds."

"Sure," I said.

He looked at Jean and motioned for her to come into the room.

"Are you doing school work?" she asked.

"Yeah. For some reason everyone thinks I need an ed-u-ma-ca-tion." I hated myself immediately. Why was I playing the dunce? Was being a gimp not enough? Was I going for pity?

Dr. Dreesen stopped my internal head banging. "Gordy is going home soon."

"I am?"

Jean smiled. She must have been familiar with the doc's underdeveloped sense of humor.

"I talked to your folks this morning. They are getting everything set up for you there. So, we won't have your company much longer."

I grabbed the doc's hand and shook it, but my smile was directed at Jean. When he finally left the room, I could not stop smiling.

"How long have you been here?" Jean asked.

"Since forever."

"Congratulations. You live far?"

"Perryville. It's only about 60 miles. One way."

Jean pulled a chair up to the table, folded her tiny, creamy hands in her lap. "Go ahead and finish. Is that algebra?"

"Yeah. It's kind of interesting, I guess."

Jean rose from her chair and walked to the window. She watched the front of the hospital for a few minutes. She was patient, I'll give her that. With only three more problems to finish, I threw down my pencil. "Done," I said.

Jean looked over her shoulder. "Good," she said.

"So, how do you know Doc Dreesen?" I asked.

"He saved my life," she said.

"Mine, too. I guess that's his job. Hey, do you want some juice or water? I feel like rolling down to the nurses' station for something to drink."

"I know where to get chocolate milk," Jean said, cocking her head slightly.

"Where?"

"There's a refrigerator in the employee lunch room. They keep it for the little kids."

I turned my chair around to face the door. "What are we waiting for?" I said. I slapped my legs and said, "Hop on."

"Not a good idea," she said.

"Come on, sit on my lap. I won't feel a thing."

Jean took a step back. Her eyes darted left then right, looking for the best path around me and out of the room. I recognized Jean's expression: the frightened indecision of a cornered animal. If I said anything more, she would bolt. I was the coyote this time, and she, the little fox kit.

My hands were poised over the wheels of the chair. I pulled back gently on the wheels, easing the chair back a few inches, clearing a path for Jean. She ran to the door and disappeared. The current created in the air by her movement smelled of citrus. I felt a stirring in my lower body, familiar but faint. I touched my inner thigh to be certain. It was just the beginning, but there was no mistaking an erection.

Nice going, I thought. It must have been a world, no, a universal record for boy meets girl, girl runs away from boy. I hoped she would not tell the doc that I tried to molest her. If I weren't in this chair I would never ask a girl to sit on my lap. Oh well, I would be gone from St. Anthony's in a few days and would never have to set foot in St. Louis again for the rest of my life. *Really nice going, McCann.*

Gordy told his nurse he wanted to see me. When I had a couple of minutes, I stopped by his room. He was in a hole of his own making, pouting about how Jean was a nice girl so she could not be interested in him.

"You never know. Some people you have to give a second chance," I said.

No response. I tried again to cheer him up, "Why don't you go outside? Explore, breathe fresh air."

He just shrugged, so I shrugged back and said, "Suit yourself. I figured you for more of the adventurous type."

He changed the subject. "Have you seen Perryville High School? It's two stories. Stairs up and down."

"They must have a service elevator somewhere," I said.

"Swell. I'll make friends with the janitor," Gordy said.

An idea dropped into my head. It was unconventional, could prove embarrassing, but certainly not really unethical. I moved to the window and looked down on the front drive, slowly nodding my head. *What do you think, St. Anthony?* I thought. I did not hear any opposition from the old guy, so I said, "Who do you think is the faster runner? Me or Clayton?"

He thought for about two seconds. "Clayton's younger, but you are leaner. Why?"

"I'll race you from one end of the circle drive to the other and back," I said.

Gordy joined me at the window. There was a huge circular drive in front of the hospital starting from one end of Chippewa at Grand Avenue to the other end at Arkansas Avenue.

"How far is it from one end of the drive to the other?" Gordy pondered aloud.

"It's about 480 feet. I've walked it many nights to think about my patients. From one end to the other and back would be less than a quarter mile," I said.

I leaned toward the window again and scrutinized the driveway once more. "What are we racing for?" I asked. "Winner treats loser to ice cream in the cafeteria?"

"I was thinking of something bigger," Gordy said with a smirk.

"Such as?"

"I was thinking we could race for pinks," Gordy answered.

I wondered if he meant pink underwear or pink hair, maybe. "What kind of pinks are you thinking about?" Gordy grinned. At first, I felt glad to see him so cheerful. Then my heart nearly stopped.

"Pinks. You know, vehicle ownership papers. This sleek wheelchair for your automobile. Winner takes all."

My heart kicked back in at fourth gear. I coughed and said, "I don't think your parents would go for that."

"We won't tell them," Gordy purred.

That relieved me somewhat. If Gordy did win, he could not drive a car. Not yet, at least.

"Deal," I said.

We shook hands. Gordy's arm and wrist muscles were admirable. My confidence was restored, at least as far as my being a physician.

I had been outside in the chair plenty of times. Clayton had me practice transfers from the chair to a car seat. We practiced curbs in the parking lot. You have to keep your center of gravity in the right place. Lean back and lift the front wheels. Big push on the wheels to mount the curb, then quickly lean forward to bring the front wheels down to the pavement. It's all about timing, speed control, and weight shifting.

Clayton told me, "The partnership of the human and his chair is pure choreography." He surprised me sometimes, but he never shocked me. Clayton was unique. I can't say I never thought of him as queer or a fairy, though I'm ashamed to admit it. But I never felt weird when he massaged my legs. Clayton taught me how to perform the most intimate bodily functions. I talked to him about sex without giggling or blushing. I came to realize that life must be tough for Clayton, not just because he was black. He had to hide who he was and be so careful about what he said or how he moved. He had his own choreography. I may have had to make a lot of adjustments in how I lived my life, but I did not have to be afraid or hide myself. Not that hiding a wheelchair was even a possibility.

Clayton suggested a few practice laps of the driveway before the big race. He wanted me to get familiar with the sidewalk. Wheels run differently on different surfaces. He wanted me to get used to the cracks and the curves. I couldn't picture taking a curve at top speed without tipping over. All I could see was a wheelchair on one wheel, burning rubber until it fell onto its side. "It's all about leaning to one side or the other. Weight distribution," Clayton said. "Meet me at the front door after my shift. Don't be late, 4:30 sharp."

At the appointed hour, I was stretching my arms by the front door when I saw Jean walking up the sidewalk. I pushed myself to the side of the door. She was on her way to see the doc, of course. If she had not complained about me yet, I did not want to give her a reminder.

Jean pushed open the front door. Straight ahead of her, she saw Clayton.

"Hello, beautiful. You made it. We're practicing. The race is tomorrow," Clayton said.

"Thanks for calling me. I thought I could be a cheerleader. Where's Gordy?" she asked.

Clayton pointed to Jean's left. She looked at me and blushed the prettiest pink I ever saw. I rolled out of the corner. I smiled at Jean and thanked her quite formally for coming to wish me well in the upcoming event. I thought I sounded like a regular Cary Grant. She laughed, but I thought I did pretty well for a nervous knucklehead.

The appointed day for the "race" arrived. Jean walked into my office unannounced and saw me in my lab coat. I appeared to not be wearing trousers. One hand flew straight to her mouth to cover any escaping laughter. In the other hand was what looked like a plate wrapped in aluminum foil.

"I'm wearing shorts, kiddo. What have you got there?" I asked.

"Cookies," she said. "I made them myself." She removed the foil and proudly displayed a dozen sugar cookies decorated with piped frosting depicting the hub and spokes of a wheel in deep green. "They are wheel cookies. I made them for Gordy."

"Very nice. How did you get here?" I asked.

"On the wings of love," she said. Then, she doubled over in laughter. I reminded myself how good it was to see Jean laugh, even at my expense.

When she regained her breath and her voice, Jean said, "I came on the bus, of course."

"I won't ask you who you'll be cheering for," I said.

"I'm sure Gordy is going to win," she said. "That is, if you want any of these cookies."

"My dear young lady, I would not throw this race even for one of your hand-crafted delicacies. Besides, I strongly doubt I will have to."

Jean left a cookie on my desk and trotted out of my office door.

I went to the physical therapy room to stretch a bit. Clayton was there, gathering towels and water bottles.

"Clayton, as your boss, I have a quick question. How should I approach the race?"

"Run like hell, Doc," he said.

"I hear there might be some wagers on this race," I said.

"I would never bet against my boss," he said. "You're going to let Gordy win, aren't you?"

I straightened my back and grasped the lapels of my lab coat in a show of professional indignation. "A gentleman never pulls a punch," I declared.

Clayton pivoted like a soldier and walked out of my office. I swear he was humming the old Depression anthem, "We're in the Money."

The biggest surprise of the day was when I looked out the window. A dozen spectators had gathered on the lawn in front of the hospital. I picked out Jean talking to Gordy. I wondered who told her about the race. Clayton's name immediately came to mind.

Clayton had a blast setting up the race. By that, I mean taking bets. He promised to split his winnings with me. The doc was being a good sport about the whole thing. "I hope you don't get into trouble about this," I said to Clayton.

"Are you kidding? You've raised the morale of this place 100 percent," he laughed.

He handed me a pair of satin running shorts, bright blue with little red stripes.

"Do you have a pair for the doc?"

Clayton rubbed his palms together. "I've got something for the boss. Just wait."

The whole hospital, patients and staff, was either standing outside on the grass or peering out from a front window. I rolled down the ramp in front of the building to cheers. They were cheering for me! I never got so much fan love when I could actually play baseball or run real track. Were they here to watch me tip the chair into the driveway and lay sprawled on the pavement with my legs bent at crazy angles? Did they expect me to lose control of the chair completely and roll off like a runaway stagecoach into Chippewa Avenue?

I wheeled up and down the sidewalk in front of the hospital, warming up for the big event. Clayton reminded me that I could lose valuable seconds at the turnaround at the end of the driveway. He suggested letting the grass slow me down. I had practiced letting the right wheel roll on the grass, with the left wheel moving faster on the pavement. The chair practically turned itself. Of course, then I had both wheels on the grass. I had to lean forward and pull the wheels with all my strength to get enough speed to return to the sidewalk. My idea was to stop, roll backward a few feet, slow the left tire, and turn 180 degrees to the right.

"With the doc on the outside lane, you will be turning in front of him," Clayton said.

"Right," I said. "Being the compassionate healer, he won't want to run into me, so I'll be able to pull ahead at least a little bit, for a little while."

Clayton made his *I'm so proud of you* expression. "Now you're talking," he said.

Dr. Dreesen walked out of the hospital wearing what appeared to be nothing but a lab coat. Sister Alison, acting as his coach, removed the white jacket dramatically to reveal the doctor's running costume. The spectators laughed and applauded. Doc wore a dress shirt and tie tucked into satin running shorts. As we took our positions at the corner of Chippewa and Grand, Sister Alison opened an old, black, cracked leather doctor's case and pulled out a pair of ankle weights from the physical therapy equipment room. Now, the small crowd laughed even louder and began to applaud. Traffic on Chippewa Avenue slowed to a crawl.

The doc laced up the ankle weights. He made a big show of struggling to lift his feet. Then we stood (and sat) next to each other on the starting line. Sister Alison used a kazoo to start the race. Off I flew at 3 mph. The doc was ahead of me. He pretended to get tangled in his ankle weights and made a couple of circles trying to get free. I passed him easily, as planned.

My turn strategy at the Arkansas Avenue end of the circle drive worked like a dream. I took the lead and held it. Clayton later told me that the doc stopped at one point and pulled a stethoscope out from behind his necktie and checked his own heart. It was enough to give me the victory and the audience. Cars stopped to watch and blew their horns.

Dr. Dreesen congratulated me with grand gestures. I asked him where his car was parked. "I ride the bus," he said. *No wonder he agreed to race for pinks*, I thought.

Was it the greatest day of my life? Up to that point, I guess it was. Of course, what goes up must come down.

I expected to be discharged after winning the race against a fully functioning biped. (Clayton taught me that term.) Uncle Konnie and his crew had been working on getting the house gimp-ready, and I decided to collect all the junk I had acquired in my time at St. Tony's. When who should appear bright and early but Roger. I pulled myself up on the trapeze bar and flung myself into my chair. "Where is your Elmer Fudd hat?" I asked.

"In the car. I figured no one in this joint would laugh at me. They see worse than me every day," he said.

"Thanks."

"Not you, of course. Come on, let's get out of here and find a milkshake. Any good places around here?" Roger asked.

I rolled toward the door of my room where Roger stood. "You drove 60 miles to buy me a milkshake?" I asked.

"Who says I'm buying?"

We found a drive-in not far from the hospital. Roger ordered the shakes, and we drank them in his car. He reached across me and opened the glove box. He pulled out a copy of the *Perryville Scene* and folded it to the "Local Doin's" page. "This came out yesterday," he said.

I read a few lines from a little box at the bottom of the page.

Local boy wins race. Gordan McCann defeated Dr. Alger Dreesen in

a foot race at St. Anthony's Hospital, the famous polio hospital in South

St. Louis. McCann was racing in a wheelchair due to a shooting accident several weeks ago. Nice goin', Gordy.

"How did they get this?" I asked.

"Search me."

"Okay, well nobody reads this stuff."

"When your mom read it, she blew a gasket. Your dad got picked up for drunk and disorderly in the front yard."

"How do you know?"

"Julie called me. She was crying. She asked me to pick her up on the corner and drive her to her aunt's house."

"Crap. Uncle Jim knows now," I said.

My milkshake started to taste like bad gravy.

"Least of your worries," he continued. "Phil is bringing your mom to pick you up tomorrow. She's on the warpath, son. She says the doc humiliated you and acted unprofessionally. Blah, blah. Julie thinks she's going to make a big stink."

Roger slurped the last of his milkshake and threw the empty cup into the back seat. He grabbed my neglected cup and finished my shake for me.

"This is not good," I said.

"You've been in a cocoon here at the hospital. Your family is losing it. Your Uncle Konnie tries to keep everything cool. Wait until you see the swell bathroom he built for you off the dining room."

I pounded the back of my head on the top of my seat. Roger started his engine. "Let me drive you home. Avoid all this mess. Your mom isn't mad at you."

"She will be if I ride home with you."

Roger grasped the steering wheel, reached over his seat with his orangutan arm, and retrieved his hat. Pulling the earflaps down, he said, "Where to?"

"Me, to the hospital. You, back to Perryville. Buy Julie a shake."

"Are you sure?" he asked, backing out of the drive-in stall.

"I've got to pack and warn the doc about Mom. Damn, why can't they stay out of this? It happened to me. I'm the one whose whole life got messed up, not theirs."

Roger shifted from reverse to second gear. When he released the clutch, the car lurched forward and we took off with a roar. When we cleared the parking lot, he turned to me and said, "Think again, man. It happened to all of them."

22

PHIL

It was the night before Gordy came home from the hospital. I drove over to the house to give a last look at the bathroom. To make sure everything was just right. I measured the door and the distance between the wall and the toilet. I pulled on the railing by the toilet to make sure it was solid.

Ida was sitting in the kitchen. She invited me in for a beer. I went into the kitchen, thinking Henry would be there, but Ida was alone.

"The old boy gone to bed already?" I asked.

Ida smirked. "He's out somewhere feeling sorry for himself. He goes out after dark. I find him the next morning in the new house, asleep on the floor or in his car."

"He's ate up with guilt," I said. "I'll find him."

"If you do find him, tell him his boss called again wanting to know when they can expect him back at work. Here's the message: 'Don't come back to work until you are steady enough to do the job.' How's that for tact? He said 'steady' instead of 'sober.' Or did I misunderstand? Oh well, just give Henry whatever message you want."

I found Henry where I expected to find him. He was at Cinque Hommes Creek, crawling through the leaves under a little stand of cottonwood trees. He was as drunk as I wished I was.

"What are you doing out here?"

"Looking for a bullet," he sneered.

"In the dark? I told the sheriff it was me."

Henry stood up and tried to lunge at me. "Stop being my loyal puppy. I don't need your help. You don't owe me anything from the war at all."

"But I have nothing to lose," I said.

"Because you don't try to get anything. You have no family, so you borrow mine. How many women turned you down?"

Henry drew back his right fist. He nearly fell on his face trying to swing at me. He tried again and hit me on the shoulder. He still fell on his face. I turned and walked toward my truck, only a few steps, and then I stopped and walked back. "Here's what I came to tell you. The shirt factory is fixing to bring in a new G.M. from headquarters."

"The V.P. himself told me to take all the time I needed," Henry whined.

"Did he say he would hold your job forever? Suck it up, Sarge."

"You know nothing about what I've lost," he said.

I knew what I was losing—patience, and fast. "Did you get shot? Are you stuck in a wheelchair for the rest of your life? It happened to Gordy. So, you can wallow around in the wet leaves or be a father to your son. If you can't or won't, then Konnie and me are ready to step up."

"Oh, you and Konnie have discussed me? The two of you?"

"Do you even know what Konnie has done? He paid his own workers from Modern Home to work on your house. People from your job volunteered, too. I helped build Gordy's bathroom. Vivian and Julie made his curtains."

I walked fast toward my truck. It was parked behind Henry's car. He stopped me and grabbed my shoulders. Between sobs, he said, "I'll do better. I'll work harder and help finish the house. I'll help Ida more and spend time with Julie. I can do more. I can be better."

I let him finish and patted him on the back. Then I reached into his car and took the keys. "Walk home. It'll sober you up. If you aren't there when I come to work on the house tomorrow, I'll come and find you again."

The next morning, I lit out early for Henry's place. It was Gordy's big homecoming day. Ida called me to say she found Henry asleep on the front porch when she woke up.

"You'll have to drive me to pick up Gordy at the hospital. You can drive Henry's car. That will solve two problems, actually. My husband is not in fit shape to drive a car. That's problem one. If I have to drive all the way to St. Louis with that man, it would likely lead to divorce if not murder. That would be problem number two."

I could not say no to a lady in need and remain a gentleman.

When I arrived to pick up Ida, Konnie had one crew putting the finishing touches on Gordy's *boudoir* in the dining room and another crew working on the new house. All the rough-in work was done and the walls were going up. Eileen and Ida had made coffee in a big urn they borrowed from the Baptist church. Even Jim was there. I made him help carry the dining room table out to the porch so the gals could feed the volunteers lunch.

I said "good morning" to the workmen. I knew most of them from working on their trucks at one time or another.

"Where's Henry?" I asked Konnie.

"Down in the cellar," he said.

I looked toward the cellar. Henry was just walking up the stairs carrying a five-gallon bucket of drywall plaster. I waved to him.

"Hey, hey," he said. "Grab this bucket, will you? I'll bring up the tape and the trowels."

"On it, Sarge," I said.

"We want to get all the walls up this weekend. We all have to go back to work on Monday."

To this day, not a word has passed between us about the night before.

23

DR. DREESEN

As I do with all my spinal cord injury patients before they leave the hospital, I had "the talk" with Gordy. It goes something like this:

"After an acute spinal cord lesion, nearly all patients have a symptom called spinal shock a few weeks after their injury. That includes patients with incomplete transections. The reflex impulses coming from the spinal cord below the level of injury go haywire for a while. This includes the reflex to empty a full bladder.

"At first, a patient's reflex related to filling the bladder with urine doesn't work properly. When the bladder is full, the reflex to empty the bladder does not automatically kick in. The patient thinks, 'Oh, this voiding business isn't a big deal. I hardly ever feel like I have to pee.' With time—and that time varies depending on the severity of the injury—motor reactions to external stimuli gradually reappear, starting with the recovery of deep tendon reflexes. Often the first reflex to return is a plantar reflex in the foot.

"Spinal shock can last for a few days or as much as 12

weeks. When the reflexes begin to return, it is nearly always in an exaggerated or spastic form. The reflex of bladder activity typically occurs as involuntary voiding. The bulbocavernosus reflex settles down in a few days. The return of sensory function is nearly always true for patients with incomplete spinal cord injuries."

Gordy waited several seconds to see if I had more to say. Satisfied that no more information was coming, he said, "Does this mean I'm going to pee my pants when I get home?"

"Maybe, for a short time," I said. "Use a catheter to void until the autonomic reflex returns. Shouldn't be very long."

"Oh, so I'll only be in diapers for a few days," he said.

"No diapers. You will get through the period of spinal shock if you understand it and know what to do."

"Is that it?" he asked.

"Well, it's interesting that spinal shock only occurs in upper primates," I said.

"No, it's not interesting," Gordy said. "The fact that you find it interesting is kind of weird, Doc."

24

GORDY

Discharge Day, at last. Clayton arrived early to say goodbye. "Now, I'll be around to your house once you are settled. You have a two-story, so we can work on some ways to get around there."

"My pop says he wants to build a new house, all on one level."

Clayton stood with his fists on his hips, shaking his head slowly from side to side. "If you aren't the luckiest pup I ever saw. Well, I'm coming to visit anyway. Until the new house is finished, you're going to have to deal with stairs. Where is the bathroom located? Up or down?"

"It's upstairs, but my uncle has built a bathroom for me under the stairs on the first floor."

"Well, until you get used to things and build up more strength for your transfers, I'm going to recommend you use a portable commode. Just for the present," Clayton said.

I batted the trapeze bar with my fist. The chain jangled loudly. I thought it was quite appropriate, the rattle of chains.

"I'll be sleeping in the dining room, you know. I doubt anyone will want to eat next to my potty chair."

"And here I was thinking what a smart, brave kid you are," Clayton said. "I'm just going to tell you the truth—there will be some embarrassing moments. I won't lie to you. But you, Gordon McCann, have the power to overcome them and make people see you and not the chair."

Clayton started gathering my clothes and belongings into a pillowcase. There was nothing left to say. It was all on me now. Whining wasn't going to solve anything, only make me more dependent.

Before he left, Clayton handed me a piece of Wrigley's gum. I shook my head at the meager gesture. He showed the stick to me and pointed to the phone number he had written on the wrapper. "Door's open day and night," he said.

I was all packed and eager to hit the road. My clothes and school books were in a suitcase. And then there was the wheelchair, of course. I had another box for everything else, mostly model cars, comic books, and candy visitors brought me. Clayton gave me a couple of woven straps to use for my exercises. I put one in my pocket and the other one in the box. I had made a few items in art therapy: a drawing of a weeping willow tree as seen through the window of the art room and a clay ashtray in the shape of a turtle with a dent in the top of his shell for butts. I finished off the last of Jean's cookies and rolled out of Room 312 for good.

I heard Mom's voice at the nurse's station. I buttoned my shirt and rolled out to meet her, but she was not there. Sister Alison pointed to Dr. Dreesen's office. I looked through the window over her shoulder and saw Uncle Phil waiting in Pop's car by himself.

"Your mother asked to see Dr. Dreesen," Sister Alison said.

"Signing me out, huh?"

"Actually, she had a complaint. I'll help you bring your things out of your room. We can set them on the floor here, next to the counter," she said.

We finished stacking the boxes. I thanked Sister Alison with a hug and headed for the doc's office. As I came closer, I identified Mom's angry voice through the closed door. The doc was speaking in a low, professional tone. "I assure you, Mrs. McCann, there was no intention to mock or humiliate Gordon in any way."

"How else could a 'foot race' with a crippled boy in a wheelchair be interpreted?"

I knocked and called "wide door," in case anyone was standing close to it. I would have to swing it open all the way to get my chair through. The doc needed to be rescued, so I swung wide the door and entered the office. He was standing behind his desk. He had cleared the comfortable chair so Mom could sit. Normally, the chair was piled with files and medical magazines.

"Here he is now," Mom said. She was standing beside the comfortable chair. When she sat down, the afternoon sun pouring through the single window in the office landed right in her face. Mom squinted and returned to her feet. With her face squeezed in the light, she could not look as if she wanted the doc's head on a platter.

Doc spoke to me. "Your hometown paper mentioned our little race. Your mother was just showing the article to me. Did you by chance give them the item, Gordy?"

I pretended ignorance of the offending article. "Not me. Clayton is your best suspect," I said.

Mom pulled herself up to her full height. "I demand an apology to Gordon in my presence," she said.

"For what?" I asked.

"Quiet, dear. Dr. Dreesen had no right to make a public spectacle of you."

"I wasn't a spectacle, was I, Doc? Anyway, it was the newspaper that called it a foot race, not anybody here," I said.

"Oh, I've spoken to the editor already."

"Mrs. McCann, I assure you that Gordy was a hero, not a spectacle. Actually, I was the one embarrassed at my performance, and I quite enjoyed it," he said. "I wish you would sit down, Mrs. McCann. Would you like a cup of coffee or tea? I can ring for a nurse."

The only time I remember feeling the temperature drop so quickly was in a winter squall.

"Taking advantage of a wounded boy, barely recovered from being shot, after two surgeries—neither of which seemed to help him much."

"They saved my life," I said.

Mom carefully set her purse into the empty chair. She was collecting herself. "I intend to write a letter to the head of this hospital. I'm sure you more than breached your code of ethics with this little display the other day."

Dr. Dreesen reached for a pen and said, "Let me write down his name for you."

I swear I could see the doc's frosty breath as he exhaled.

I stepped in, so to speak. "Mom, the race was my idea. I wanted to test my chair skills before going home. I never expected anyone would watch us, much less write about it in the paper. The doc only agreed to the race to raise my spirits. I was nervous about going home, managing on my own. Besides, I won."

Mom was still fuming, but at least her breathing had slowed.

Dr. Dreesen said, "He beat me fair and square, ma'am."

"Well, as long as Gordon isn't set back by the incident, I will take the matter no further."

"I'm fine, Mom. Let's get out of here and let the doc get back to taking care of people who need him."

I rolled a tight 180 and headed for the door. I did not turn to see if Mom followed me but kept rolling to the nurses' station. Uncle Phil was holding my suitcase and box, chatting with Sister Alison. Mom joined us, and Sister Alison came out from behind her counter and gave Mom a hug. "He'll be fine, Mrs. McCann. I'll keep praying for him, nevertheless."

Then Sister Alison leaned down close to me. She whispered a soft prayer and rubbed my flat top. "For luck," she said.

Uncle Phil opened the back door of the car. I lifted my butt from the chair and pushed up with one fist on the chair seat and the other on the seat of the car. Uncle Phil gave me a little nudge, which I did not need. I scooted into the seat, gripping the headrest of the seat in front of me.

"He did it," Uncle Phil whispered.

With the chair folded and stowed in the trunk, a chill ran through me from my neck to my hips. I was on my own now. I leaned to the right and looked up into the rearview mirror. I watched the hospital shrink into the past, further and further behind me. Nervous? More like terrified.

25

PHIL

We stopped at a diner on Highway 61 near Imperial. I was about dying for a cigarette, but Ida didn't allow smoking in the car. Ida wanted to go into the diner first, to see if there was room for a wheelchair. As soon as she turned her back, I opened the car door, jumped out, and lit up in one smooth motion.

The parking lot was gravel. The diner looked like it had been dropped via helicopter into the middle of the forest. The trees came right up to it. It smelled good: wood smoke and BBQ.

Gordy leaned out of the back window, resting his chin on his folded arms. "What's up with Pop?" he asked.

"Oh, he's blaming himself for what happened to you. I've told him over and over that I'm sure it was my bullet that hit you, no offense. I said, 'Henry, stop and think. Who was the better shot in the Army?' He's just ate up with guilt. Insists on working on the house every night until all hours. Then, he drops into a sleeping bag right there in the unfinished house."

"I had no idea," he said.

I threw down the finished butt and continued, "I told him, 'Henry, you're risking your job carrying on this way.' He hardly sleeps, and when he does, it's because he's passed out drunk. I'm sorry to burden you this way. Maybe you can forgive him because he's never going to forgive himself."

I can't figure what came over me to tell all that to Gordy. It was true enough, but I should have kept my mouth shut. It's a family matter and none of my business.

Ida returned from the diner. "Anybody want coffee? It looks pretty clean. They've got some nice-looking pies." I'll say one thing for Mrs. McCann: when she's through being mad, she settles down quick.

I opened the trunk and lifted Gordy's chair out. "I hope one of those pies is cherry and they've got *la-mode* to go with it," I said. Gordy got himself into the chair smooth as could be. I winked at him. "That means ice cream. I learned that word in Belgium, where they speak French for some reason." I guess I was always willing to make a fool of myself for a McCann.

26

GORDY

There was one step up to the door of the diner. I climbed it with ease. I asked Mom to order a hot fudge sundae for me and rolled off in the direction of the restrooms.

The door to the men's room was too narrow for my chair. The wheels might have cleared the door frame, but there was no room for my hands. No matter how I turned, I could not squeeze through the door. After many attempts, I examined the room. There was space enough for my chair in the little closet. The sink was close enough to the toilet that I could use it to brace myself to transfer to the seat. I just could not get through the door. There had to be a way. Uncle Phil or—God forbid—Mom would show up soon to check on me. *Think, Gordy.*

I still had the woven strap Clayton gave me in my pocket. By scooting my butt forward in the chair seat and leaning forward, I could toss the doubled strap across the sink faucet and pull myself in.

Attempt Number One: I missed the faucet completely.

Attempt Number Two: The strap snared the top of the faucet spout then slipped off. Attempts Numbers Three - Six: Same thing.

Attempt Number Seven: The strap landed around the spout. I slid it up close to the brace of the spout, where it was the strongest, and pulled slowly. I was in! If Clayton could see me now!

Afterward, I realized there was nothing outside the bathroom for me to lasso and pull myself out. Here is where the improvising genius came into play. I drew the strap under the seat of my chair. It was a folding model, so by pulling up on both ends of the strap—one on each side of the seat—I could squeeze the sides of the chair together just an inch. I quickly locked the strap and rolled out of the bathroom like a pro. The whole operation took only about fifteen minutes. I would have to work on bringing my time down. Still, I was damned proud I did not pee my pants or call for help. So cool!

My first night home, Mom insisted on no visitors. However, that didn't stop my neighbors and friends of my folks from coming by to welcome me home the next morning and all afternoon right up until dinner time. They all said the same thing: how sorry they were for what had happened to me, and how proud they were of my progress so far. Each and every one of them brought at least one plate, bowl, or platter of food. I counted two cakes, several gelatin fruit salads shaped like wreaths or lobsters (for some reason), a potato salad, some coleslaw, jars of pickles sweet and dill, a smoked country ham, entire loaves of bread, and little pieces of cheese rolled up in sandwich meats and stabbed with a toothpick. By the time Mom turned off the porch light, the old dining room table was groaning. I estimated that if we all ate one serving of 3 or 4 dishes every day, the food would last us about three and a half weeks. I heard Mom call her sisters and tell them under no circumstances were they to bring food to the welcome-home party planned for the next night.

Pop came and went all evening. So many things to check on in the new house. He spoke less every time he returned to the house. Julie whispered to me that Pop smelled like Wild Turkey. He was so jittery—up and down in one chair and then another, I was glad when he went to turn out the lights in the new house. We did not see him again until morning. Julie said he slept out there most nights.

The dining room between the living room and the kitchen was the biggest room on the first floor of the old farmhouse. At the back of the room were stairs to the second-floor bedrooms. Opposite the stairs was a set of three large windows. The table was cherry wood, at least a hundred years old, with two removable leaves that made it big enough for twelve people. I guess Grandma McCann needed the room to feed her big family and farm hands. Now the table was pushed close to the big windows. The leaves of the table stood propped against a wall. There were four chairs at the table, the rest stacked next to the leaves. "The arrangement is only temporary," Mom told all the guests. "Just until the new house is ready."

On the other side of the room was my bedroom. Behind a heavy curtain hung on an amazing chain-and-bar setupwas my own bed. A trapeze bar hung over the bed, from a frame attached to the headboard. The "room" was completed with a small cabinet for clothes, one of the dining room chairs for visitors, and a portable commode. Even though Uncle Konnie had made a cool bathroom for me, Mom insisted on the commode until I worked out the choreography of moving from bed to chair to bathroom to toilet. I had mastered this in the hospital, but remembering the doc's explanation of spinal shock, I decided to keep the commode until I was certain all my faculties had returned.

Sleeping in the dining room was very weird at first. The sound of my movements echoed with no carpet to block sound. The rattle of the trapeze chain sounded like Marley's ghost (from the Dickens story, except louder) every time I changed positions in the night. The glow of the streetlight on the corner flowed through the triple windows and over the top of my privacy curtain. The stairs creaked when, one by one, the family came down to the kitchen for a glass of water. In short, man was not meant to sleep in dining rooms.

I had not returned home to the house I grew up in and left on the morning of April 24th to hunt a turkey. I slept in the wrong place. Furniture was in the wrong place. Everything was temporary, and home is not temporary. The house no longer welcomed or comforted me. I had lost my only refuge. I had lost life as I knew it; everything was insistently not the same. I could not escape to the baseball field to be with my friends. My sense of independence was deflated. No more walking to a friend's house or biking to the movies in town. Forget wandering off, sneaking away, disappearing for a few hours. Hell, even upstairs was out of reach. I was incarcerated without the possibility of solitary. My bathroom door did not close tightly when my chair was in the way. When I used it, I was keenly aware that my pissing, farting, and flushing could be heard by one and all.

Yet, in my oh-so-public life, I felt lonely. I stayed behind my curtain or outside, out of the way of people walking through rooms, up the stairs, down the stairs. Everyone was on the go except me.

27

PHIL

Konnie made good on his promise to build a bathroom under the stairs. I wouldn't have thought it possible to build a usable bathroom in such a cramped space, but build it he did. Konnie said the advantage was that Gordy would always be in a sitting position, so the ceiling did not have to be very high. Also, he would only need it until the new house could be finished. He showed up early one morning with his toolbox and one of his employees. I know he paid the guy from his own pocket, but he never said a word about it or asked for any reimbursement. I'm sure he paid for all the fixtures, too.

I swear, I never saw a shower so ingenious as the one Konnie built for Gordy. It was about half the height of a regular shower. When I first saw the frame for it, I said, "Konnie, what were you thinking?" But he showed me where the grab bars would go so that Gordy could slide himself onto the built-in stool and shower away from a spray only about five feet off the floor.

Aside from Gordy needing his own place to bathe and such,

another reason to get Gordy's bathroom finished was Julie. She threw a conniption about the commode next to Gordy's bed in the dining room. I had witnessed her tantrums many times. This one was brutal.

"I'm not going to eat in a room where there is a toilet," she said. "You can't make me. It is unhealthy and probably against the law."

Ida tried to explain that it would only be for a few days while Gordy got used to maneuvering his way in and out of his new bathroom.

"I want my own bathroom, too. I don't want to share with you and Daddy anymore. It stinks after Daddy uses it for number two, and his whiskers are always in the sink."

"This is good training for when you get married," I said. Not helpful.

Ida tried to show Julie how there was an advantage for her. "You can use the downstairs bathroom, too. It's not only for Gordy."

"Gross!" she screamed dramatically.

Ida pointed out that lots of children in the world have no indoor bathroom at all. "Why, my parents grew up using an outhouse on the farm."

"Yeah, but this is 1955, not pioneer days."

Yeah, Julie was pretty much a pill in those days. I understood, even if I hated seeing the family in turmoil when they already had so much to worry about. I could see that she had gone from being the family's little princess to the kitten who refuses to use the litter box. You still love the little fur ball, even when you want to strangle her.

Henry was a whole other story. I loved the sarge like a blood brother, and my heart broke for him. I thought for sure once Gordy was home and Henry could see how well he was doing, he might ease up on himself a little. No sir, just the opposite. Henry started showing up at Earl's Petroleum or at my house, drunk as a skunk in a trunk. Earl's method of dealing with Henry was to offer him more drinks until he was passed out cold and then throw an old raincoat over him, lock up the office, and go home.

Ida was strict about no company on Gordy's first night home. She even sent me packing after I dropped off Henry, who headed straight for the cellar of the new house. But that family was about the partying-est bunch I ever saw. The next day the phone lines started jingling, and by supper time, the guests were arriving.

I was late for the party. I had nothing to bring for the table, so I picked up some ice cream on the way. I could only afford two pints, but at least I wasn't empty-handed. When I got to the house, I held out my ice cream to Ida. She smiled and said a "thank you" that was way out of proportion to the gift. She turned to Julie and asked her to carry the ice cream into the kitchen.

"Have Gordy do it. It's his party," she said.

"You know very well why not," Ida whispered. "You have two working legs."

Julie didn't budge. "Well, my legs have been carrying things all day, and they are tired. I don't have any wheels, in case you haven't noticed."

I took the ice cream into the kitchen myself. *Somebody needs to downshift the sass,* I thought.

Gordy sat at the end of the dinner table, sort of. The arms of his wheelchair were too high to let him roll under the table even a little ways, so Ida set up a card table at the end of the regular table for him. It was awkward, but he insisted it was fine. I could tell my boy wasn't happy about all the attention this accommodation made for him. When Ida asked if the table was sturdy enough for his plate, he snapped. "It's fine, Mom. Sit down and eat."

Roger joked that Gordy should invent a wheelchair that had a scissor lift under the seat, so he could ratchet himself up. "I saw something like that in a cartoon once," he said. I laughed and said Gordy and Roger could make a fortune with the adjustable chair and not have to go back to school. I did my imitation of Bugs Bunny: "Eh, what's up, Doc?" Then, the twins had to try, competing back and forth for the loudest version.

In the back and forth, one of the twins upset his glass of milk. "Knock it off," Gordy barked at the boys. Eileen mopped it up with her napkin and canceled dessert for poor Landis and Jefferson.

Ida had gone all out, bless her. She set the table with her best cloth napkins. They were pretty with little violets embroidered in one corner, but they were the devil to keep on the lap. I stuffed the corner of mine into my pants pocket. Gordy did not think of that, and his napkin slid off onto the floor. He leaned over the arm of his chair to pick it up.

Ida hollered, "Gordy, stop." She thought he was about to tip his wheelchair, I guess. She jumped up from the table and ran to the card table. She picked up the napkin from the floor and tucked it into Gordy's shirt and smoothed it over his chest like he was two years old. "That's better," she said, and returned to her seat. Gordy yanked the napkin out of his shirt and laid it beside his plate.

As for Henry, he was as big a mess as ever I saw him. He ate very little and spoke not a word. At some point, he just got up and took his plate into the kitchen to eat. He never looked at Gordy one time.

When everyone had eaten their fill (or more), Ida said, "Let's get the table cleared and have dessert."

Roger jumped up and ran outside. He returned in half a minute with a piece of lumber about three feet long. This he set across the arms of Gordy's chair and started stacking dishes on it. Everyone except Gordy laughed as the dishes rose higher and higher. The ladies feared the worst for their beloved dishes, but Roger assured them that this would save them so many steps they would thank him later. It worked, too. Gordy couldn't push his wheels, of course. He kept the dishes steady, and Roger wheeled him into the kitchen and unloaded the dishes onto the counter by the sink. Vivian clapped her hands. Her husband scowled at her and said, "Don't encourage them."

Gordy returned from the kitchen carrying two cakes on the board across his wheelchair. Konnie said, "Now I understand the English expression 'room and board.'" That guy was a prince. Gordy did not find it amusing at all. "I'm doing this once and once only. I'm not a dumbwaiter." Jim began to explain that Gordy had used the word incorrectly, but he was drowned out by the calls for different desserts from around the table.

Ida brought other desserts to the table: a pie, strawberry shortcake, and my two pints of ice cream. When Gordy asked for strawberry ice cream with his cake, Ida looked down at him and said, "Remember, you aren't as active as you once were. Best go easy on the sweets from now on or you'll get so fat you won't fit in your chair."

The room fell silent. Gordy pushed himself away from the table and rolled to his "bedroom." Julie suggested we eat dessert outside, which we did. Strangest party I ever attended.

28

GORDY

I stayed in my bedroom until everyone left with their desserts for the yard. I then picked up a pint of ice cream and a spoon from the dining room table and returned to my room. Since Landis and Jefferson had been denied dessert, they came to find me. At the foot of my bed was a pile of gifts neighbors had brought the day before. The boys couldn't keep their eyes off of them, so I let them look through the pile. As they examined each comic book, game, or toy, one or both of them said, "Wow" or "Cool" or "Lucky duck."

"You can each pick one thing," I said. "Not the View Master or the wood burning kit. Your mom would have a cow if she saw you with that."

Roger parted the two pieces of the curtain and put his head inside. He was wearing his fur hat. Mom had made him take it off at the table (fearing something might crawl out of it, no doubt). He growled so loudly that the twins took him for a bear and started to scream. I told them to keep it down or they'd not get to have something from my gift collection. Roger came in and sat on my bed and finished the carton of strawberry ice cream.

Julie appeared just then, drawn away from the Great Digestion going on in the yard among the adults. She pulled the curtain aside and poked her face into my bedroom. "What are you doing in here? Don't bother Gordy," she said.

"Gordy said we could each choose something," Landis said.

I pointed to the mess the boys had made. "You can have something, too," I said. "What do you want?"

Julie pointed to the commode, partially covered with dirty clothes, and said, "I want that toilet out of the dining room."

The twins had not noticed the commode before Julie pointed it out. After seeing it, they ran from behind the curtain, screaming, giggling, and wiggling, saying "eww" and "gross."

With the table cleared, Mom and the aunts went into the kitchen to clean up the dishes. Julie joined them to observe. The twins were reading comic books in the living room. Roger and I joined the men outside. Pop was missing, of course. Uncle Jim pulled himself up in his chair and looked at me as if he'd noticed me for the first time all evening. "Well, hello Gordy. Nice of you to join us. You get around in that chair like a champ."

"Thanks," I muttered.

"I've just been talking with Konnie about how you're going to navigate that contraption around the high school building come fall."

"I'll be fine," I said.

"We can't move all your classes to the first floor. Too disruptive," Uncle Jim said.

Uncle Konnie answered for me, "There is a service elevator in the building. You can give him permission to use that."

"I'm not principal yet," Uncle Jim chuckled. By that he meant his evil plot to get rid of the current principal—whatever it was—had not yet been successful.

"I can get into the building from the teacher's parking lot," I offered. "The elevator is right inside that back door."

"You'll have to take a look at the width of classroom doors and restrooms," Uncle Konnie said. "I would be glad to help."

Uncle Jim scratched his chin and shook his head. "The problem is, as always, the budget. Where will we find the funds to pay for those kinds of changes for just one student? Naturally, I'll do everything I can to convince the school board."

Once again, Uncle Jim had positioned himself as pitcher on the team. The game can't go on without him. He and only he can convince the school board to allow the poor crippled boy to finish high school.

"I'm not worried," I said. "I'll write letters to the school board members myself. They are supposed to be on my side. Don't forget, Roger Pardee is my best friend. It would be a shame if he decided to give up baseball to spend time with his crippled friend."

Roger grinned at Uncle Jim from under his coonskin cap.

We sat quietly for a while and let night fall over our shoulders. It was a cool, comforting darkness. Behind us, the lights in the house brightened. The new house faded into shadows. Uncle Jim set up a chair for Pop. "In case he decides to return tonight," he said. What an ass. If the kids at his school knew half of how he acted at home, they would hate him even more. If possible.

Uncle Konnie stretched and said, "I have hired a designer for the company. It's only part-time for now."

"Designer? What for?" Uncle Jim snorted.

"Women contribute a lot to the decision to buy a new house. They spend the most time there, after all."

"It's your business, I guess," Uncle Jim said. "You must be doing pretty well to offer such frills as a designer."

"Yes, business is good. Families are growing. People are moving away from the cities. They want to raise their children in small towns, but close to the city's advantages."

Uncle Jim shook his head.

I said, "You know who would be great at that job? Aunt Viv. She's so creative and artistic. She knows what the ladies want."

Uncle Jim laughed. "Son, half the time your Aunt Vivie doesn't even know what *she* wants until I tell her."

"She knows," said Uncle Konnie. "That's why I hired her."

At just that moment, peals of laughter rang through the living room window. Mom and the aunts were watching *Beat the Clock* on television. Poor Uncle Jim. He thought everything was about him. He stood up and looked around in the darkness. "Time for us to head on home. Excuse me, gentlemen." He reached down and shook my hand. "You are a brave young man, Gordon. You're going to get through this, you'll see. I wouldn't be surprised if you walk into school this fall and don't even need to bother the school board. What does your doctor say?"

"No chance," I said.

"Doctors don't know everything," he mumbled as he walked toward the house.

Uncle Konnie gave my arm a squeeze. "Neither does he."

A hospital is a place where people go to get better or to die. No other outcomes are available, right? Even a woman who goes to a hospital to have a baby leaves "cured" of her pregnancy. Based on that, since I did not die from being shot and having two operations, it followed that as long as I was in St. Anthony's, I was getting better. Right? The nurses, Clayton, and Sister Alison all said I was a good patient and would do very well long term. Even Dr. Dreesen gave me a semi-smile sometimes, a sign of optimism.

The truth was, it felt like they were all in on the trick. A hospital isn't where people get better; it's designed to make the patient *believe* he is better than when they came in. The halls are vast. The floors are smooth and uncarpeted. Even an idiot could operate a wheelchair in that environment. The doors are wide and open with the slightest push. Some doors even push in and out. It all gives the wheelchair patient a feeling of false security. No such doors exist in the outside world. But boy, do hospitals spare no effort to give the patient the illusion that he can learn to take care of himself, clean rooms and hushed halls aside.

I fell for it all. I lapped up the praise of the nurses. I believed Clayton when he tilted his head and said, "That was a great effort. Can you do a couple more for me?" I always did two more or whatever else he asked of me. I so wanted to make this stranger proud. That's the kind of power these experts have over a poor jerk like me. Heck, I usually gave him three more reps just to earn his "Way to go, Champ." Clayton probably said the same thing to guys so messed up they had to blink once for "yes" and twice for "no."

The reward for all my healing was to go "home." Where the doors were narrow, tables too high, where Mom's precious throw rugs bunched up between the little front wheels of my stroller. Excuse me, I mean my wheelchair. Where I go to shit in the dining room behind a curtain. I saw my options as either to decline into decrepitude or to play the happy fool so everyone else could feel good.

Thus began the period of my depression. Maybe it was also fear and worry for the future. After the initial jubilation of my return home, I fell silent and brooding. I went through several stages, as follows:

Stage One: Seething in Silence. The Wizard of Oz said, "Pay no attention to the man behind the curtain." I stayed in my curtain cave, alone, all the time. Mom did her household chores. Julie played with dolls, listened to the radio, ran back and forth through the dining room. No one was allowed in my "bedroom," not even Roger. When I refused to roll myself the few feet to the dining room table for lunch, Mom lifted the bottom corner of my fabric barricade and slid a sandwich on a plate to me.

I refused to attend church because there were a thousand steps into the building. While the family worshiped, including sometimes even Pop, I stayed behind. Once I said an earnest prayer for healing. Nothing happened. What I could not figure out was why God had it in for me. I lay in bed on stinky sheets I refused to let my mother wash. If being crippled was to be my lot, I did not care to fight it.

One night, Pop came home drunk (again). He could not make it all the way to the second-floor bathroom, so he puked in my toilet. When he passed by my bed on his way out, he said, "This room stinks." That was it. I had hit bottom, hard. Out of respect for Mom—and her alone—I cleaned up the room and asked to be served lunch in the kitchen with her and Julie.

Stage Two: Profound Profanity. I felt justified to curse in response to the injustice done to me. I called my legs *damned* useless. I complained that my wheelchair was *shitty*. I even told Clayton on a visit that my trapeze was a *crappy* monkey toy. I announced to the world that because of some *bastard* coyote, my life was FUBAR (*fucked beyond all recognition!*). Uncle Phil taught me that last one.

One day, one of the front caster wheels of my chair got caught in a rolled-up corner of one of Mom's throw rugs in the dining room. I cussed a blue streak to get untangled. I jerked so hard on one of the hand rims that the chair started to tip. I shifted my weight in time to keep from ending up on the floor, but not before calling the rug a motherfucker. Mom started crying in the kitchen. Julie ran from her upstairs bedroom down to the dining room. She threw the throw rug over my head and punched it hard with her fists.

"Stop cussing in Mom's house. Dad hurts her enough. Behave!" she yelled.

When Julie was beating the rug on my head, it loosened some dust. I started to sneeze and choke. I pushed and pulled, finally getting the rug off my head. I was alone. Mom and Julie had gone outside to take dry clothes off the line. They each held one end of a sheet and walked toward each other, folding it in half. Then, they folded it again the same way. I used to do that with Mom. I sure wasn't her "helper boy" anymore. I wanted to be, more than anything.

Stage Three: The Expert. This was when I bored everyone with my extensive knowledge of spinal cord injuries, or, as we in the know call them, SCIs. I lectured the mailman, the men working on the new house, and even strangers in the grocery store—anyone who would listen. One day, Roger and I were playing Monopoly on the porch. I started my master class on the bulbocavernosus reflex when he stood up and said, "Paging Dr. Schweitzer. Are you going to buy the Short Line Railroad or not?"

Stage Four: Alfred E. Newman. This was the stage when I adopted the attitude of "What, *me* worry?" It occurred to me that no matter how hard I tried, I would never be a success now. So why try at all? I stopped doing my exercises. I whined until Mom waited on me just to shut me up. Even Julie preferred to do little chores for me rather than listen to me blubber about all I had lost. If Clayton ever gave up on me, I would've been sunk. I saw a future where my wheelchair was my only friend. Up to now, I had refused to name it, but I could just about hear me saying, "Well, Clementine, let's roll into the living room and see who Lawrence Welk has on this week."

Stage Five: Resignation and Acceptance. Dr. Dreesen told me not to beat myself up over little setbacks because they were sure to come. "They taught us in medical school that everyone does the best they can every day." I could live with that. My apologies to everyone I dragged through my pity trip.

I added my own Stage Six: Get over it. Find something you can excel at, and show it off every chance you get.

A few weeks after my welcome home party, I woke up behind my iron curtain to an unfamiliar feeling. In the short time I had been without useful legs, I became used to sleeping on my back or on my side with my legs out straight. Unless I woke up in the night, the position I fell asleep in was my position when I woke up. This morning, I felt my legs bent, tucked toward my chest. I hadn't slept on my left side with my legs tucked since before the accident. How did I bend my legs in the night when I can't move them when I am awake? Yet, when I pulled my blanket off my legs, there they were, as straight as when I arranged them the night before, with a pillow between them to keep my back straight. As soon as I saw my legs, the sensation that they were bent disappeared. Still being pretty new to my condition, I shrugged it off. I anticipated discovering more complications and indignities in the future.

This bent-leg phenomenon happened several more times. I woke up feeling bent legs. Once, sitting in my chair outside in the shade, I dozed off. This time, when I woke up, I felt my legs were out straight like I was sitting on the ground with my back against a tree. I refused to open my eyes. I liked feeling my legs, straight, bent, or tied in a bow. I raised my arms to stretch and felt my legs stretch. Finally, I opened my eyes and there they were—the traitors—bent legs.

I wanted to call the doc immediately, if not sooner. But let's be real—would a doctor see a fifteen-year-old patient without his parents? Not likely. And waiting for Clayton's next visit would be torture. I could have been worse by then: my feet facing backward or my knees bending the wrong way. So, I decided to ask for the next best thing: permission to call Clayton. I wanted to get his advice on increasing some of my therapy repetitions ASAP. Permission granted.

After our call, I told my mom that Clayton wanted to see me back at St. Anthony's before changing my exercise routine. She said I should ask Dad.

"I'll drive you," he mumbled in that tone of martyrdom a parent uses when they agree to do something for a kid that they don't want to do. I had not asked him to drive me to St. Louis, and I never would have asked him.

"No need. Roger will drive me," I said. "You've got work and the new house."

"I won't have you on the highway without an adult."

"Roger is nearly eighteen." (In another eleven months.)

"I meant an experienced driver," Pop said.

"Roger has been driving for two years. He got his license back in February." My math was a little off, but Pop didn't notice.

"Not good enough," he said.

I kept trying. "Roger can borrow his dad's very safe car for one day."

"Try to always have at least one rich friend," he said.

Mr. Pardee was not rich, but he was a generous guy. I thought I had made some progress with Pop, so I kept going. "You know Roger. He's smart and responsible. He's captain of the baseball team."

"It's not Roger I object to," Pop said. "There are lots of adults who shouldn't be allowed behind the wheel. They don't pay attention to what they are doing. They get distracted by the smallest thing. They drive too fast, pass on the solid yellow line, fall asleep. I know how a tiny mistake can mean disaster."

I couldn't tell Pop that he had just described his own driving since he started getting drunk every night. I didn't want to hurt him. He had to fight his guilt on his own. If I focused on my recovery, maybe he would get the idea.

"So, Roger is okay?" I needed that extra clarification.

Pop was wearing down, I could tell. "I just don't want to get a phone call that you are lying in a ditch somewhere, unconscious, with God knows what kind of injuries. Or worse." His voice was intense if not loud. He retained enough control to not let Mom hear him. He thrust his head forward and threw the words at me. His eyes were open wide, but his hands were closed in tight fists on the arms of his chair.

I reached out and covered his fists with my hands. "I never blamed you, Pop. I never will."

I kissed the top of his head. Roger was right. It did not happen only to me. But Pop's pain was beyond fixing by anyone but himself.

29

GORDY

"I see why they named this place 'White Castle,'" Roger said as we entered the little restaurant. The white tile from floor to ceiling was dazzling. I entered the door at the corner with no problem. Jean had recommended we meet there for hamburgers. The White Castle was close to a bus stop, so she wouldn't have to walk far. We found a table where my chair was not in the way. Roger got more stares than I did. He was wearing his Elmer Fudd hat.

While we waited for Jean, Roger said, "I'll check out the bathroom situation."

I knew what he meant. He was looking out for obstacles for me. He had taken the job upon himself. "Latrine reconnaissance," he called it. I felt pretty confident I could get into most public bathrooms. There was always an element of challenge. The important thing was not to wait until the last minute. Choreography takes time.

I fidgeted as I waited for Jean. I wiped crumbs off the table, patted down my hair, and twisted my head around to look at the door so many times that it was stiff the rest of the day.

Seeing her smile when she saw me was like the end of a storm. I would not have been surprised at all if a rainbow had appeared over her head.

When Roger returned from his mission, Jean was sitting with me at the table. He ordered a bag of a dozen tiny hamburgers and Cokes for all.

"Remember Roger?" I asked Jean when he finally joined us.

"I remember the hat," she said.

Jean looked beautiful. Her hair picked up the light reflecting off the tile walls. As she turned her head, a golden sheen moved around her brown curls.

"What are you doing for the summer?" Roger asked Jean.

"Looking for a job. I need new clothes for school. My high school is full of cake eaters, you know? Kids with money. I have to work hard to make an impression."

"Not for me," I said.

Roger said, "You should transfer to Perryville. You would be Homecoming Queen. I'd make all the football team vote for you."

"Thanks, guys." Jean blushed. Copper hair flecked with gold, pink cheeks, and an angel's voice. How much could a guy stand?

We gobbled up the burgers. Roger suggested we find a place to park and talk more. After I conducted my own successful latrine mission, Jean guided us to a little park. It was nice in the shade. After some friendly chatter, Roger excused himself. He had brought the leftover White Castle bag with him and wanted nothing more than to find some birds to feed—whether they were hungry or not.

"I miss you," I said to Jean. We sat close together in the back seat. Two teenagers in the back seat of a parked car. How normal could we get?

I put my arm around her shoulders. We kissed. I scooted my butt and arranged my legs so we could face each other. Jean put her hand gently on my right knee, just above the knee. "Can you feel that?" she whispered.

"Of course," I said. "Just not the way you think. There's no sensation of touch or heat from your hand, but I feel it in a different way. I am aware of a softness around me. Like floating on water or maybe a cloud. Sounds goofy, I guess."

"I'm glad, because I feel very good being close to you."

Roger gifted us an hour. He offered Jean a ride home. She asked to be dropped at a bus stop. She made me promise to call her, "Just for five minutes."

Roger dropped Jean at the bus stop, and we headed to St. Anthony's Hospital. "Sounds like you're in a long-distance romance, son. Maybe you better find a job."

30

DR. DREESEN

I got a word from Clayton that Gordon was coming in to see him. I asked Clayton to send him my way when he was finished. Gordon was waiting in my office when I arrived—late—for our appointment. He looked wonderful: well-rested, focused, good eye contact, and generally pretty damned normal for a fifteen-year-old kid.

"Sorry to be late," I said, as I tossed some files from my desk onto a chair. I wanted to show full attention to the patient. Later, Sister Alison would help me find the files that slid off the chair onto the floor.

"No need to apologize," he said. "You're a busy man."

"Are your parents with you?" I asked.

"Nope. My friend Roger drove me."

Here was independence on a scale I had not expected.

"We had lunch with Jean. The three of us," he said.

All was clear now.

"So, do you have some questions for me or concerns? You seem to be handling the chair quite well."

"I'm a regular wheel man," Gordon beamed. What a great kid.

"What's up, then?"

Gordon pulled a little notebook from under his legs. In it, he had taken measurements of the circumference of his legs at different levels between hip and foot.

"I noticed when I was here some of the patients had pretty limp pant legs. Their legs were pretty much skin and bones. I promised myself to never have stick legs. I use a towel to pull on my feet and flex my calf muscles the way Clayton showed me. To exercise my thigh muscles, I sit on the edge of my bed, my legs hanging over the mattress. I hook the top of a crutch over my toes and pull up with my gluteus muscles. Of course, the crutch barely moves, but I work up a sweat. What do you think about my numbers?"

"Very impressive," I said. No trophy, no gold medal. I did not want to give him the slightest impression that he could avoid further atrophy. "We need to get you into a standing position for at least a few minutes every day."

"You mean on crutches?" he asked.

"Not crutches. The point of being upright is to maintain good circulation. Blood clots develop in people who sit all the time."

"So, what should I do?" he asked.

"Some people suspend themselves in a harness of some kind, on a door or a tilting board."

"Like in the movie Frankenstein?"

I laughed. "Why not? Just strap yourself in and let gravity do all the work."

"You want me to hang from a hook on the back of a door like a bathrobe or a raincoat?"

"No, like a person trying to stay as healthy as he can in every way he can." After our race, I got a lot of razzing from the hospital staff. Today, I was playing it very professionally.

"There's one other thing, Doc," Gordy said. "Some mornings—this is going to sound crazy—I switch up my sleeping position to prevent bed sores—Clayton showed me how to put a pillow between my legs when I'm on my side—either left side or right side."

"Very good. Maybe we should fire Clayton and hire you." I tried to make a joke.

"This is serious, Doc. Let me tell it. Some mornings, after I've slept on my left side, I feel like my legs are bent up to my chest. That's how I used to sleep. You know, old Gordy."

"How long does this sensation last?" I asked.

"Just until I look at my legs and see they are in the same position I put them in the night before."

"Do you get feelings like this at other times?"

"No. Just when I first wake up. Sometimes, I put off looking at my legs as long as I can. I like the feeling of normal legs, I guess. Who wouldn't?"

I explained that what Gordy was experiencing was known as phantom limb. It's very common with amputees. They often feel as if the limb they lost is still there. The severed nerves at the amputation site continue to send signals to the brain. Often, they are pain signals. Phantom pain is another term for it, but usually, spinal cord patients don't have pain.

"So, it's not a sign that my legs are trying to come back?" Gordy asked.

"I'm afraid not. You will not have phantom limb feelings forever."

Gordy was starting to drop his eyes as I spoke. I hated taking the wind out of his sails. "Be sure to go downstairs and see Clayton before you leave," I said. "He will have some good ideas about rigging up a way to suspend yourself. Start with a few minutes a day and build up to half an hour at least."

"What am I supposed to do while I'm suspended?" he asked.

"Whatever you can. Not much, obviously. Listen to the radio, sing, look out a window if you have one close, practice math in your head. Pray. Meditate," I suggested.

"What's that?" he asked.

"Oh, it's like clearing your mind by focusing on something. Stare at a candle flame or a tree. Just watch it without thinking about anything. It's very relaxing, and the mental rest is good for the body," I explained.

Gordy's hands were still in his lap. He had not reached down to the hand rims on his chair in preparation to leave. There was more he needed to say.

"Doc, I want you to take the bullet out of me."

"No, Gordy. I promise you that the bullet won't move or hurt you any more than it already has."

"I don't care if it isn't necessary medically. I need that bullet."

"Why?"

"My pop is drowning in guilt. I say drowning because he's drinking a lot. Too much."

"Was this a problem before?" I asked.

"Nothing like this. He disappears in the evening and comes home at the crack of dawn to take a shower and go to work. I hear him sometimes in the kitchen, drinking coffee in the dark. He mumbles. Uncle Phil told Mom that if he comes to work drunk one more time, they'll fire him. If I can show him the bullet, prove to him that it came from Uncle Phil's gun, then he will stop trying to destroy himself."

I walked across the room to my office door. I saw Sister Alison walking toward me with a file in her hand. I shook my head and closed the door.

"Gordy, I can't perform an operation that has no benefit to my patient. It's unethical and dangerous."

"The FBI has a lab where they can look at a bullet and tell for sure if it was fired from a certain gun."

"Yes, I've had some experience with ballistics testing. But the FBI will not investigate an accident. There was no legal crime."

"What if I paid for the operation myself?" he asked. His desperation to save his family was heartbreaking.

"I took an oath: 'Do no harm.' An unnecessary operation could harm you, and I won't risk all the great progress you have made."

Gordy nodded and reached for the wheels on his chair. He was finished talking.

"Would it help if I talked to your father?" I asked.

"No. If Uncle Phil can't get through to him, no one can. They were Army buddies in the war. That's some kind of sacred bond."

"I'm sorry, Gordy. Call me if you want to talk more about your dad. I have some contacts at the V.A. Hospital. Let me see if there is someone there he could talk to about his feelings."

Gordy rolled down the hall to Sister Alison's desk. He asked her to call Clayton and see if he was free to answer some questions.

In the reception area, Roger was reading a magazine. He appeared to have an animal on his head. I returned to my office. In a couple of minutes, I heard Clayton's voice. "Aren't you a sight for sore eyes! Did the doc challenge you to another race?"

"I need your advice on how to hang myself," Gordy said.

Clayton laughed and said, "I think you mean suspend yourself, my man."

That kid is going to make it, I thought.

31

GORDY

Uncle Konnie installed a door to the kitchen to keep the light and noise out of my room. That was good, because he widened the opening when he installed the jamb. I could now easily roll into the kitchen. He also put up real walls around my *boudoir*, so I was no longer an offense to the first floor. Julie didn't complain about eating in the dining room. Pop was rarely there for meals anymore.

"Mom, I want to move the old wardrobe into my bedroom," I said one day at breakfast.

"You have a dresser," she said.

"It's too small. Roger said he could move it downstairs for me."

"I want the wardrobe," Julie said.

"You have a closet, remember?" That was me to Julie.

"No need for rudeness," Mom said.

"That wasn't rudeness. I'm just asking for the wardrobe, which is in my bedroom, anyway."

"You get everything," Julie shouted.

"Name one thing," I said.

"Your own bathroom."

"Everyone complained about my portable commode, but I can bring it back anytime."

"Gordon!"

"Sorry, Mom. Could I get another glass of milk?"

"Julie, pour your brother another glass of milk, please."

Julie opened her mouth to complain, but I rolled my chair back and opened the refrigerator door. I filled my glass on the table with milk and returned the bottle to the fridge.

Julie clapped her hands. "See, the great Gordy can wait on himself."

"We knew that, Miss Smarty. I was asking you to do a kind thing for your only brother. You may want him to do a kind thing for you someday," Mom said. She said it without much conviction or emotion. She was bored with telling us the same things over and over. She was also worn out with worry about Pop. How could she not be? He was either at work or out drinking most of the time. She had to take care of everything for everyone. She was allowed to lose her temper, in my book.

Julie and I caught each other's eyes and held the stare. Mom collected our dishes from the table and set them in the sink.

"Do you want some help with the dishes, Mom?" Julie said.

"No," she said without turning to look at us. "Just leave me alone for a while. Go watch television, go play with your friends, go outside. Don't come back until I call you for lunch. Not one second before I call you. I love you both, but go. Now."

32

GORDY

One thing I learned from sleeping in the dining room was that when people sleep, their house wakes up. Sleeping upstairs in the back bedroom, I grew up ignorant of the sounds of the night. The noise of a person walking down the stairs, even on tiptoe, was like a bullfrog croaking. When I first came home from the hospital, Mom crept downstairs to check on me nightly. I became an expert in the nuances of her steps. There was an inhale sound when a foot pushed down on the wood, then a different note for the exhale when the foot lifted. There was a branch that tapped on the kitchen window when the wind was strong.

You could say I made a study of the expanding/contracting cycle of old wood in our house. Then one night, I heard a new sound. It was in the dining room for sure. Buzz—drop. Buzz—drop. The buzzing was like torture. The sound of something dropping was a tease to make me think whatever was buzzing had landed. Somewhere.

Come late May, a bullfrog woke me up in the wee hours. I

heard a kitchen cabinet door open and close. A chair scraped the floor. That's when the buzzing started. I endured as long as I could, but I had to know who was in the kitchen and what was buzzing.

"Pop?" I said as I rolled into the dark kitchen.

"Did I wake you, son? I just came down for some cold water," he said. He was clearly drinking from a can. It wasn't that dark. Why lie about a late-night beer?

"Sorry I woke you," he whispered.

"It wasn't you, Pop. Don't you hear that buzzing sound?" I asked.

We both strained our listening powers. It wasn't so loud in the kitchen, but we both heard it. Buzz—drop. Pop laughed. "Don't you know what that is?"

"No clue."

Pop took a sip of "cold water" from his can and asked me, "What comes around every thirteen years?" he said.

I shrugged. He smiled too much for a simple little riddle. "Cicadas. There's probably one or two caught between the screen and the window. They fly around, buzzing, looking for a way out."

"You mean those bugs that leave their dead skins on tree bark?"

"The very ones."

"Should we try to save it? Set it free?" I asked.

Pop crossed his arms on the table and lowered his head. I heard him crying. Another sound of the night. I didn't know what to say, so I just waited. Maybe this was a joke about the poor trapped cicadas. What did I know?

Without raising his head, Pop sniffed a few times and said, "I'm sorry" about ten times. I rolled a little closer to him and rubbed his shoulder. "Not your fault," I said. "I don't blame you."

Pop pulled his head off the table but did not look at me.

"You should," he said. "If it helps, you can hate me for the rest of your life."

"Never!" I said.

Pop grabbed a paper napkin out of the little rack on the table. He dried his face and blew his nose. In the quiet, we heard the cicada buzzing. Pop cleared his throat and looked at me. "There are two kinds of cicadas. One group comes out of the ground every thirteen years. The other comes out every seventeen years."

"What do they do in between?" I asked. This might be a good thing. When Pop gets going explaining stuff like animals or weather, he feels good.

"Who knows? The adults fly in a big swarm. I mean, thousands upon thousands. They eat, mate, and lay eggs in the ground. Then they die."

"You mean it takes thirteen or seventeen for the eggs to hatch?" I asked.

"That's right."

"So, while they are in the ground, are they dead or alive?"

"It's very interesting. There was a good article in the Missouri Conservationist about cicadas since 1955 is the end of a thirteen-year cycle. Let's rescue the one caught in the screen. You can get a close look at it."

Pop jumped up from his chair and pushed me into the dining room. I had zero interest in a bug that sleeps for thirteen years, wakes up, gets laid, then winks out. Leave it to Pop to be an expert on something so goofy. I hoped that he finally believed that I did not blame him for my accident. I really needed some normal stuff to keep my mind off what I had lost. Besides, I thought it was his job to comfort me. Oh, well, cicadas it was.

33

GORDY

Julie liked to sit on the stairs when Clayton made a physical therapy house call. When he was in a good mood, Clayton could be pretty funny. Julie liked his jokes, especially how much Clayton himself laughed at them.

I was sitting under the door of my bathroom after exhausting myself with eight pull-ups on the bar across the top of the doorway.

"Miss Julie, wasn't I in this very house two weeks ago?" Clayton rubbed his forehead and squeezed his eyebrows together, pretending to try to remember.

"You sure were," Julie said.

"Son, you accomplished *almost* eight pull-ups today. Are you practicing at all between my visits?" Clayton asked.

"I sure do. Sometimes I do twenty or twenty-five," I said. "Give or take."

Julie jumped up from the stair. "Now, you're fibbing. You barely get to ten, maybe twelve." She turned to Clayton and batted her eyes. "Gordy made me his official counter."

"Yeah, to get you to leave me alone the rest of the time."

Clayton had heard enough. I half expected him to shake his head and declare, "Kids say the craziest things." Instead, his jaw muscles were pulsing like a no vacancy sign at a motel. Julie was loving it; Clayton was about to flip his lid. Instead, he picked up his equipment bag and pivoted to face me.

"This is not a game, Gordon. I have taught you the choreography. It's up to you to do the dance. If you don't maintain your muscle mass, you will lose it. You'll lose the strength to make transfers and lie in bed in your mama's dining room until she is too old to feed you and wipe your butt."

Then he turned to Julie. "That's when sister takes over."

Mom walked into the room, hands on hips, as Julie was screaming and stumbling up the stairs. She had heard everything from the kitchen. She greeted Clayton and walked him to the front door, where the two of them talked in low voices. Finally, Clayton nodded and left with a smile from Mom.

As the front door closed, Mom lost the smile and walked toward me. I was still in the bathroom doorway. My mouth was hanging open and my eyes were filling up fast.

"I don't know who I'm going to put out of the house first, your father or you, Gordy," she said.

"Nice going, Gord-o. You've hurt the one person you can always and forever count on to love you and put up with your crap," I told myself.

Mom continued, "I have been so proud of how you accepted what has happened to you. You tried your best to do everything asked of you. Now you play around and waste Clayton's time after he comes all this way to help you."

That hurt. "I'm sorry, Mom. You're right. I guess I'm feeling a little sorry for myself."

"You're entitled," she said.

I pointed toward the living room. "Wouldn't you be more comfortable sitting down?" I asked.

Mom walked around to the back of my chair and pushed me into the living room. She parked me at the end of the sofa, so we could talk quietly, side by side. "I'll work harder, Mom. I promise."

A son should not make his mother cry, ever. I felt like an ungrateful jerk. She faced me and took my hands. "It's not you, Gordy. I know you do your best. Life has dumped a big load of manure on you, and you're allowed to slide a little once in a while. It's your father I worry about most. He's about to lose himself, and I don't know how to help him. Sometimes, I want to tell him to go on and live in the new house. We'll stay here until he gets himself straightened out."

I surprised myself by saying, "That's actually a good idea, for now. You need some peace and quiet. Let Uncle Phil handle Pop. He's about the only one who can. I'll handle myself," I said.

Mom wiped her eyes and almost smiled. "I guess that leaves me with Julie," she said.

"She's not such a bad kid. She's kind of the cow's tail in all this. She doesn't know how to help, and she's probably afraid of what will happen to her. Let Aunt Viv handle Julie."

Where did that wisdom come from? When I had legs, I was always moving from one thing to another. From my seated position, I saw more and listened more to the people around me.

Mom kissed my forehead. "Okay, back to reality. Which should I make, Snickerdoodles or brownies?"

34

PHIL

I was about to go nuts trying to save Henry. He was running his marriage and his relationship with Gordy into the ground. He was fixin' to lose his job too if he didn't straighten himself up. He drank too damned much for a man with a job and a family. I told him so; even offered to handle his drinking along with my own. Alas, his sense of humor was mostly shot, too.

I called my friend, Burl. He was a farmer near Centralia who offered me work when I needed it. There was always a machine that needed attention on his place. Burl knew everyone in central Missouri. I asked if he knew a taxidermist near Perryville, preferably one who didn't mind telling a story now and again.

Burl was glad to help. "I know one guy not far from you. He's out on Highway T, before you cross the bridge over the South Fork Saline Creek. Name's Emmett Grider. He's a good guy, even if he served in the Navy. I'll give him a shout on the short wave and let him know what you're planning."

Now, I had to convince Henry to take a Sunday trip with me to see a man about a tiller he wanted to sell. Ida was a stickler for attending church every Sunday, especially now that the Lord had saved Gordy's life. If Henry was hungover, as he frequently was on Sunday, she did not encourage him to accompany the family. If my plan worked, I figured God would forgive me the lie.

Saturday morning before our trip, I picked out a not-quite ripe honeydew melon from my garden. I examined it carefully for size and density. At my workbench in the garage, I stirred up a bucket of plaster of Paris. I dipped the melon into the plaster and set it on an upturned coffee can to dry while I listened to the Cardinals game on the radio. When the plaster had dried enough to be sticky, I dipped it again. It took a long time for the plaster to build up the thickness of a coyote skull. After applying the final coat, I placed two washers on the globe to represent eyes. Coyote eyes, to be precise.

I had bought a box of rifle ammunition—Federal .22 Cal, 40g—what Henry had used. I positioned the plaster melon head on top of an old barrel in the brush behind my garden. The melon was at the same height as a stalking coyote's head. Then I paced backward the distance Henry and I had stood from the coyote back in April. When I was satisfied that I had recreated the scene at Cinque Hommes Creek as accurately as I could remember, I fired a shot right between the two washers. The melon did not explode, but it did fall off the barrel. "Got you, you son of a bitch."

The bullet I fired at the melon exited out the back. In the real coyote, with her head down, the bullet could have passed into her neck. We'll never know, but for my purposes, it did not matter. I followed the trail of melon bits and found the flattened cartridge. Bingo. I wrapped the bullet in a handkerchief and made my way to Henry's house.

I drove Henry toward Bonne Terre, in Saint Francois County. It was a pretty drive in the summer. The Ozark hills were covered in trees, keeping the wind cool as it came through the truck windows. The hills are rocky and full of caverns. Lead mining was the big industry then. Farmers lived in the valleys where lots of little streams watered the land.

Henry sat silently, staring out the passenger window. I felt good about my preparation for the mission. I had talked to Burl's friend the night before and felt confident he would play along.

"How did you meet this taxidermist with a tiller for sale?" Henry asked without looking away from the window.

"My friend Burl knows him."

That answer satisfied Henry enough. He continued staring out the window. After a few more minutes, I said, "His name is Emmet Grider, and he told Burl that a fella brought him a coyote carcass that he found at Cinque Hommes back in April. He wasn't interested in having the body stuffed; he just wanted the nice winter pelt. Emmet skinned and fleshed the coyote for him. It only took a few days to dry on a stretcher, and the guy came back and picked it up."

"What did Emmet do with the skinned carcass?" Henry asked.

"Processed it for his dogs to eat."

"Have you met Emmet?" Henry asked.

"Talked to him on the phone just last night."

"I doubt it's the same coyote," Henry said. That was the

new Henry—anticipate the worst about everybody and everything.

When we arrived at the Grider farm, I said I would look in the barn and see if he was there. I also said I needed to take a piss. I counted on Henry wanting a little sip from the pint bottle in his hip pocket, and he obliged. "I'll be along when you find him," he said. This gave me time to give Emmet the bullet from the melon.

Emmet was a very friendly guy. I think Henry would have warmed up to him pretty quick if he'd been sober. Emmet showed us the tiller and named a price. After we struck a deal, I asked to see the taxidermy workshop. It was in the front of a huge old barn that he didn't use for anything other than storing several generations' worth of tools and equipment. After we were acquainted, Henry went right to the point.

"We heard you processed a she-coyote carcass back in early spring."

"Beautiful animal. Shot between the eyes. Not another mark on her. The guy who brought it in said he didn't shoot it. He was lucky to find the carcass before the hawks and crows got to it. The pelt was perfect. Are you interested? I don't know if he sold it yet, but he could easily get a couple hundred dollars for it."

"I'm more interested in the bullet you found in the animal," said Henry. His patience for chit-chat had expired.

"The bullet? What for?"

I jumped in. This question was not part of the script. "Oh, we were just curious about the caliber. If there are coyotes in that area, it doesn't hurt to carry ammunition that will put it down."

"So, did you find it or not? More important, do you have it?" Henry asked.

"I did keep it. After Phil called me last night, I dug around and found it," Emmet said. He opened a drawer in his tool cabinet and pulled out an envelope. It was an old envelope from the electric company. Emmet had written on it "May 1955 -she coyote."

"You always keep such good records?" Henry asked. He acted like the envelope had cooties or something. Wouldn't touch it.

"If the sheriff comes nosing around about an illegal kill, I want to have my ass fully covered."

"Open it up, Henry. Take a look," I said.

Henry ran his hand over the envelope. I could practically hear his heart banging inside his chest. Months of guilt and self-doubt hung over him. Ida's insinuations and Jim's condescending silence. Every person he knew, including himself, had an opinion one way or the other about whether Gordy was the victim of an unpredictable and unpreventable accident or was the poor child born to a careless, trigger-happy idiot. He'd told me one time, "If we ever find out for sure that the bullet was mine, I'll only need one more—for me."

Henry took the envelope from Emmet. "On second thought, I can live without knowing."

I stepped forward. I was mad as hell. After all the trouble I went to, and Emmett, too, I wasn't going to let Henry screw it up for me. "Well, I can't. Open it."

"I know whose bullet is in here," Henry said.

"You do?" said Emmet.

"Of course. It came from the rifle belonging to my best friend."

"How can you know that without opening the envelope?" asked Emmet. By then, he'd figured out he was in the middle of something more than just curiosity about an old bullet.

I shuddered. Now I wished I actually had taken that piss.

"I know it was you, Phil, because you got the date wrong. I shot that coyote on April 24th. Are you saying this 'guy' with no name, who can never be found, kept the carcass in his truck for more than a week before he got around to bringing it to Emmet? "

Emmet interrupted. He now had some skin in this game. "The carcass was fresh when he brought it in. I probably wrote May on the envelope because that's when I got around to putting the bullet away."

And there it was. Three men stood in the taxidermy shop, shuffling our feet in the dust. Finally, Emmet slapped me on the shoulder and said, "I need a beer. I sense there's a long story I want to hear and you need to tell. Come on into the house. The refrigerator is full and the wife is in Columbia visiting her sister."

"Sounds good to me," I said. "What do you say, Sarge?"

Before entering Emmet's house, Henry pulled me close to him by my shirt collar. "I don't ever want to hear how you did this."

Emmet turned to face us. "I sure as hell want to know. I'm guessing this was an act of pure friendship," he said.

Henry let go of my collar. "That's what you get with a knucklehead private for a best friend."

We talked and drank all afternoon. When we reluctantly parted company at dusk, after multiple cups of coffee each, Henry and I each carried a big jar of Sweet Missouri BBQ Sauce. Emmet was a cook in the Navy and he had his own line of sauce he sold around the county.

Driving home, Henry said it had been a good trip even if nothing was resolved. "I never will find the answer," he said. "I have to find a way to live with that."

"And cut back on the booze."

"One thing at a time, Private," he said.

We rode in silence for a while. The Mark Twain National

Forest was a quiet, beautiful place at night. The leaves on the giant trees danced with the moonlight, creating a peaceful shadow show.

"What if I got the date right and you had opened the envelope and found my bullet?"

"Private, neither one of us is a ballistics expert. Can you tell one flattened bullet from another?"

"No," I admitted.

"Thanks for the effort."

"That's what a good private does. He makes his best effort and leaves the heavy thinking to the officers."

35

GORDY

A few days after our trip to St. Louis, I called Roger to come over and help me with something important. When he arrived, we sat at the dining room table.

"What's up?" he said.

"Here is the deal. The doc said that my blood could be clumping together in my ankles or calves and I won't feel a thing. He said a blood clot that starts in the legs can break off and travel to my lungs or even my brain. I could end up dead."

"Kids don't get blood clots," Roger said.

"Thank you, Dr. Pardee. We have to come up with a way for me to suspend myself using what we have in the house. There is a wardrobe in my old bedroom upstairs. It's a little taller than me. We need to bring it down here. If I could somehow climb up between the doors and support myself, I might be able to get my blood flow back to normal by the time I can get something better. Clayton's working on it for me, but my blood could be bunching up as we speak."

❋

Roger moved the wardrobe out of my upstairs bedroom using a hand truck from the new house. The builders used it to move material around. Once we rearranged my dining room and set up the wardrobe, I explained my idea to Roger.

"Inside the wardrobe is a bar for hanging clothes. It might be low enough for me to grab onto. From there, I will pull myself up to the tops of the doors. I'd have to pull myself up with one arm and then let go to grab the door. Difficult but possible.

"I throw a towel over the top of each door for padding under my arms. I sit on the floor of the wardrobe under the bar. It's a stretch, but I know I can get myself up. I'll have to swing my body a little for momentum. Then, it's just a matter of letting go of the clothing rack with one hand and throwing my arm over the top of the door. Then, do the same with the other arm."

Roger saw the folly in my idea immediately. "That rack won't hold you. You don't have enough strength to pull yourself up and out to grab the doors. Yet. I can't lift you straight up. You're dead weight, no offense."

"All right, all right," I said.

"There you go." Roger was clearly relieved.

We both stared at the wardrobe, each thinking there must be a way to do this. And then the idea struck. We got one of Pop's ladders. From there, Roger would tie a rope around my waist, then pull me from behind the ladder, hoisting me up from step to step. We looked at the plan from every angle. It could work. Roger pulled me up the ladder rung by rung.

We thought we had succeeded when I reached for the tops of the two wardrobe doors, lost my balance, and fell. Roger caught the wardrobe before it landed on top of me.

❄

"Shit!" I cried out. Roger responded with, "Jesus Christ Almighty." That caught Mom's attention. She ran into my bedroom and saw me and the wardrobe on the floor.

"What on earth?" she cried.

Roger turned and said, "No time to explain. We have to take Gordy to the hospital. His shoulder may be dislocated."

Mom ran for her purse. Julie was with Aunt Viv, thankfully. Roger helped me into my chair, then from the chair into his dad's car, then out of the car at the hospital, and so on.

An X-ray showed my shoulder was not dislocated or broken. It was pretty strained, though.

"How did this happen?" the doctor asked.

"I was working on my upper body strength. I guess the weights were too heavy."

Mom nodded. "That's right. Big weights. Next time use the smaller weights, son."

"I will, Mom," I answered. I left the hospital sore, but thanks to Mom, I was not humiliated.

On the ride home, I wondered aloud what we could tell Pop and Julie. They knew I didn't have any weights at home.

"We've got all afternoon to think of something," Mom said. "I'm calling Clayton about getting you a safe suspension contraption."

The doors of the wardrobe never closed properly again. I'd bent the hinges. Not bad for a left field has-been.

❄

Clayton came through, of course, with one of those woven lawn chaise lounge chairs. The middle folded and locked into different angles for sitting, lying down, or in between. Clayton rigged it so the hinge would lock well enough for me to hold onto the top of the backrest and dangle my legs. I needed help getting out of the contraption, but someone was usually around.

Julie liked to find me when I was hanging and stood in front of me hopping from one foot to the other, scratching herself under her arms while hooting. She said it was an imitation of a monkey, but it looked more like a pretty ordinary ten-year-old sister to me.

I tried to bring Gordy a little something when I went to visit. Nothing big or expensive, just a little token. I enjoyed a relaxing read or a good comic book and thought Gordy felt the same. So, I brought Gordy the adventures of Batman, the Flash, Green Arrow, and Captain Marvel. There had been a big uproar about comics leading to juvenile delinquency the year before. Congress even got involved and made the publishers set standards. Personally, I thought it was all stupid. If the Army could have drafted a few heroes like what appeared in the comics, the war would have been over before they had to drag my ass and Henry's into it. Anyway, Gordy seemed to like them, so I kept buying them. I encouraged him to pass on the issues he had read to his friends.

One day in mid-June, I found Gordy sitting on the front porch with a comic book in his lap. He was studying the ad for Charles Atlas' program of building muscle by dynamic tension. I would like to say that I brought Gordy comic books so he could discover Charles Atlas, but that would be untrue.

"What are you studying there?" I asked.

"Do you think I could build my upper body solely sitting in this chair?" he asked.

"I think you can do anything you want. How can I help?"

That was it. We sent for the Dynamic Tension program and started doing the exercises. Gordy practiced curls for his biceps and triceps without a bar or weights. He made a schedule and kept track of how many repetitions he performed of each exercise in a little notebook. He did finger lock chest pulls, bicep curls, triceps pull downs, high elbow rolls, and triceps dips. I helped him set up one of the dining room chairs in the backyard. I dug shallow holes for the legs and set each leg in the hole of a cinder block. At first, I was worried that Gordy would lose his strength and fall. But I got some old blankets and tied them around the cinder blocks. Gordy kept inventing new exercises on his own and adding them to his routine.

Every chance I got to stop by the house, Gordy showed me his notebook. He took measurements of different muscle groups with a sewing tape measure and recorded the numbers. Day by day, the numbers increased slightly. In three weeks, he had added as much as an inch on all parts of his upper body. Gordy also measured his legs and hips. Those numbers decreased. I wanted to tear that page straight out of the notebook. But Gordy was better than any of us in facing the truth about his condition. I wonder if Gordy showed his notebook to his father. Unlikely.

"Mom threw a fit about the last phone bill," I said.

"Too many calls to Jean?" Roger asked.

He followed me into my bedroom. "How am I supposed to make money when I'm stuck on my ass in this chair?" I said. Roger lay on my bed and pulled himself up a few times on my trapeze bar.

For every pull-up Roger did, we named a job that can be done sitting down: radio disc jockey, toll booth attendant, pilot, painter as in artist, gambler, piano player. I shoved Roger off my bed and took a turn on the trapeze bar. I came up with: ticket seller at the movies (I had to forfeit that one because the little booths were too small for my chair), professional knitter, food taster, author, telephone operator.

"What we need, what we both need, is a real skill. Something we can be experts at, that will count now and all our lives," Roger said.

"You are already on the fast track to the major league. The Great Harry Carey would have to admit that much."

"Oh sure. Do you see Gillette hiring my scarred face to sell razors?"

"Maybe we could have some kind of partnership. You do the ambulatory work, and I'll just roll around," I suggested.

Roger sat in my chair and pulled it up close to the bed. "Okay. I've got two ideas. Take your pick. Chess grandmasters or professional poker players."

I completed my pull-up and dropped down onto my elbows. "Do you know how to play either one?" I asked.

"Both, as a matter of fact. A little."

"That makes you the expert. You decide."

Roger seemed to have expected this response. "Chess is cool. You're famous in one way but invisible, too."

"How's that?"

"Sidney Bernstein made $20,000 last year."

"Never heard of him. Oh, I get it."

After Roger's baseball practice, he came back to my place very excited. He carried a thick book under his arm. He set it on the dining room table next to me. I had pulled out the unopened chess set someone gave me at my welcome home party. Keeping me occupied while seated seemed to be a big concern for the grown-ups in my world.

"That's some book," I said.

"It's full of openings and famous chess games in history. Stuff we don't have to worry about now."

"Okay."

"First, you have to learn the pieces and how they move. Each one moves differently."

My confidence took its first hit. Roger set up the pieces according to the diagram on page four of the *Encyclopedia of Chess* from the Perryville Library. Chess was going to be harder than baseball, I could see that already, but I was up for it.

Playing chess is basically fighting a war. You win by making your opponent surrender. The pawns are the infantry. The officers and the King and Queen start out behind the lines. Unlike in real war, they don't stay behind but slide eventually into the thick of battle. Even the bishop—an armed chaplain, more or less—can sneak up on a knight or rook and make a kill.

After a couple of hours moving pieces diagonally, horizontally, one square at a time, even in an "L" shape, our brains were tired. "How come the Queen is the only piece that can move any way she wants?" I wondered aloud.

"Because girls get all the breaks," Roger said.

It did not take long for us to start making up our own moves for the chess pieces. That's when chess became really fun. The knights' horses jumped over rooks like a steeplechase. Pawns could encircle their king and all move as one group. The two Queens became friends. Bishops could fly. Silly things like that. In one version, we put the Kings in toy cars and raced them around the board. Most fun any young man ever had playing the game of Kings, no doubt.

The final word on chess was: Chess was serious. Chess was hard. Chess took forever to learn. Chess would not make us rich. I put the board and pieces back into the box, taped it shut with black electrician's tape, and shoved it under my bed.

Roger and I learned the game of poker in 15 minutes. Two pair beats one pair. Three and two is a full house. Straight. Flush. Easy.

We played for peanuts, literally. We paid scant attention to the game. Roger folded a full house to my bluff over a pair of threes. We played a few more hands, and then we realized we had eaten all the peanuts. The house was quiet. Mom and Dad were out shopping. Julie was occupied in her room.

"I've got a question for you," I said. After drawing four cards, I had a pair of fives and no other cards over a ten. I was full of peanuts. My winnings didn't fill an ashtray.

"Is this how you bluff? Distract the other player with questions?" asked Roger.

"No, just curious. It's kind of personal."

"Okay," said Roger.

"How did it feel to be on fire?"

Roger rearranged the cards in his hand a few times before answering. "It hurt. Not at first. When I was inside the house, I was feeling my way through the smoke. I stubbed my toe on the bed leg. I yelled about that. Meanwhile, the collar of my shirt was in flames."

"You didn't feel it?"

"Like I said, not at first. When I was dragging Mom to the window, my neck started to hurt. By the time I got to the window, my hair was flaming. Luckily there were two firemen on the porch roof. As soon as I stuck my head through the window, one of them unloaded his extinguisher on me. The other one grabbed Mom. He handed her off to a guy on the ladder and started to beat out what was left of the flames with his gloves. I still didn't know I was burning. I thought he was beating me for starting the fire, which I didn't."

"My dad said the side of your head was charred black."

"Yeah. It hurt a ton, but the worst pain was when they got me to the hospital and started pulling off the burnt skin. I screamed and swung at the doctor. I caught one nurse on the jaw with a left hook."

"Jesus!"

"She was okay. Anyway, I could not take the pain so they gave me a hypo and knocked me out."

I was silent, afraid to open my mouth in case I vomited a gut-full of peanuts. "Okay, why does the skin on the left side of your head look different in spots?" I finally asked.

"It's a bunch of pieces sewn together."

"Whose skin?"

"Mine."

"From where?" I asked.

"Different places." Roger pulled up his right sleeve. There was a square of skin on the underside of his arm whiter than the surrounding skin. "A patch came from here. Another patch came from my other arm. Inside my thighs and my butt."

"You have butt skin on your head?" I whispered. I started to laugh, tentatively at first. Then, Roger took off his Cardinals cap and shook his head. The laughter exploded at that point. After we recovered, Roger stared at me. He looked in my eyes and clenched his teeth. "Tell no one."

"Make me," I said.

"You have one friend. Care to go for zero?" Roger threatened.

"Sorry, man. I was kidding."

Roger stood and picked up his coat off the floor. It had fallen off the back of his chair when we were laughing together before. "Too late. You broke the code," he said.

"What code?"

"The freak code. Don't make fun of a fellow freak."

"I would never ..."

Roger turned his back to me. He stepped toward the living room. He was actually leaving.

❄

Make me. Was I eight years old? Did I have so many friends I could afford to lose one? I was a stupid, insensitive shit.

"Wait," I said.

Roger stopped walking but did not turn to face me.

"I know how to restore the balance," I said.

"Balance of what?"

"Of us. I'll tell you something gross about me. If one of us breaks the code, the other one will have ammunition for revenge."

Roger considered my idea. Finally, he returned to his seat, leaned toward me, and said, "It better be equally gross."

"When I first came home from the hospital, I had what they call bladder shock. I didn't feel the sensation that I had to piss. I pissed myself all the time, so I had to stick a catheter in every couple of hours to empty my bladder. I put one end of the tube in my dick and the other end into the toilet. Sometimes it took half an hour. Then I had to pull it out. Christ, what a mess."

Roger's eyes were enormous. He was sufficiently appalled. He shook his head. "Still?" he said.

"No, my bladder and bowel sensation came back."

"Bowel?"

"Yeah. I had to use suppositories at first. Sat on the can for an hour sometimes waiting to finish. A few times, I had to, sort of, dig it out."

"Damn, man."

"I'm okay now. Mostly," I said.

"Mostly?"

"Also, if I go somewhere I'm not sure about the bathroom —whether my chair will fit—so I keep a bottle in the car."

"That's way worse than having butt skin on your head," Roger said.

Check and mate.

Roger picked up the cards and tried to shuffle. His hands

were shaking, and the cards went everywhere. Roger squatted down to pick them up. The Ace of Clubs was by the right front wheel of my chair. I rolled the wheel over the card just as Roger reached out to pick it up. "I think you just found a new way to cheat," he said.

I laughed. Not a big laugh, but enough for both of us to know equilibrium had been restored.

36

GORDY

"**P**oker is not a physical skill. More practice will not help us," I argued.

Roger and I had been practicing poker every evening after he finished baseball practice, unless his mom needed him for a chore or errand. One evening, after an all-day practice, he said he was too tired to hold the cards high enough to see them. Mom asked him to at least eat dinner with us, but he said he needed to get on home. He had been eating two dinners—one with us and one his mother made when he got home. "Coach says I'm getting sluggish," he said.

I rolled outside to say goodbye and to make sure Roger got into the right car. He was dragging like a 20-year-old hound. I had been thinking about an idea to pick up Roger's spirits.

"I believe it's time we took our poker skills on the road," I said. "Can you get a car?"

"No sweat," he said.

The next day, Roger arrived in his cousin's beat-to-heck 1940 Buick. It had no trunk cover or back seat. Instead, Roger's cousin installed half a seat from a big Packard behind the driver. We drove south on County Highway B, turned onto Tanglewood Drive to Eugene's Bear Den.

The bar was set back from the few businesses at the intersection. It was a little house with weathered gray wood plank walls and a narrow porch with a wooden railing to keep drunks from falling off. Strings of red and yellow Christmas lights framed the two front windows on the inside. If this place was not pitiful, I don't know what pitiful is. This was my first time at a bar, so maybe that was normal.

I could not get into the bar, of course. Three wooden steps separated me from all the wonder inside. Roger loped up across the dirt parking lot and up the stairs to see how to get me in with the least fuss. There was a back door for deliveries, including a ramp where they rolled kegs of beer into the back room. I wheeled myself around to the back of the building and rolled up the ramp into the back door.

The exterior of the Bear Den should have alerted me to the look of the inside. Except for the Christmas lights dangling from the front windows, the place was dusk-like. Also, dust-like. The tabletops were clean. I could not tell if the floor was clean; probably the reason it was so dark.

Roger walked through the door ahead of me. He was wearing his wooly hat. The man behind the bar yelled at him, "Hey, that entrance ain't for customers." Roger stepped to the side, and I rolled in. The bartender waved us both in. He called to the dozing customer at a corner table, "Lookee here. We got us a real bear in the Bear Den today."

"Are you Eugene?" Roger asked.

"None other," Eugene laughed. The customer at the corner table had not moved.

"Where is everyone?" Roger asked.

"It's kind of early. What are you boys drinking?"

"Two beers, I guess," I said. I could not see over the bar, so I rolled back to get a view of the man's head.

"You boys both twenty-one or is it twenty-one years between the two of you?" asked Eugene. The dozing man in the corner jumped when the bartender slapped a rag on the counter at his own joke.

"What else have you got?" I asked.

"Coffee, soda pop."

"Two pops, then."

Eugene delivered two bottles of Orange Crush to the middle table in front of one of the windows. Uncle Phil said if we wanted to "scare up a poker game" we had to sit in the middle of the room. "Are you boys meeting your folks or something?" he asked.

"No, we're here on our own."

"I see. Well, the sleeping beauty at the bar is named Horace, if you can believe that. How about you hombres?"

"I'm Gordy, and this is my friend, Roger."

"Well, take off the hat, Roger, and get comfortable," Eugene said.

"He can't," I whispered. The bartender leaned down to hear me. "It's covering a medical device," I said.

Eugene nodded and touched the side of his nose. "Welcome to you both. I expect we'll get some more customers in here directly. Let me know when you need a refill." With that, Eugene returned to his place behind the bar. I noticed that he raised his eyes from his work every so often, looked over at us, and chuckled to himself.

Three Orange Crushes later, I needed to take a leak. Roger had already used the john behind the bar. "What's the pisser like?" I asked. Never before April 23, 1955, did I ever think about the condition or even the location of a bathroom. Roger reported that my chair would not fit in the bathroom. I grabbed an empty pop bottle, a handful of paper napkins, and headed for the back door. As I rolled through the storage room, I noticed something high on a wall, partially covered by a stack of boxes of empties. At first, I thought Eugene had hung up a rug on the wall or a winter coat. Then, I recognized it: a silver coyote pelt, hanging upside down.

The head hung down behind the boxes. The back legs were nailed to the wall. The tail was tucked down behind the pelt. That's probably why I did not recognize it at first for what it was. I tried to get my chair close enough to touch the fur. In the process, I knocked over a pair of ski poles propped against the wall. I reached up as far as I could. My fingertips brushed the edge of the fur that had once covered the coyote's left flank. It felt coarse, stiff, and dusty. Dead. I thought of the expression "tail tucked between its legs." It indicated cowardice, weakness in an animal. It was a demeaning posture for a powerful predator. I smirked at him stuck up on a dusty wall, out of sight, his head hanging down. He was imprisoned forever in a storage room of a crummy bar in Nowheresville, MO. I rolled down the ramp victorious toward a shed behind the bar. I pissed in the pop bottle and sat a moment in thought when finished.

It was *my* coyote on that wall. There was no doubt in my mind. I needed Roger's help to move the boxes so I could see the beast's face. How many of my dreams had that devil invaded over the last four months? How often had I sat on the front porch at dusk and surveyed the trees behind the house, watching for her or her ghost coming for me?

The she-coyote was my nemesis, my Moby Dick. Dead or alive, she vowed to pursue me, or so I thought in lonely, frightened moments. I was powerless to escape her. I could not run, climb a tree, or jump over a fence to get away from her. I imagined her walking through the woods, maybe limping, taking a cool drink from Cinque Hommes Creek, waiting for me to return. She carried a bullet, just as I did. But I had survived. More than survived, I had triumphed. I may have been forced to ride a chair and piss in pop bottles for the rest of my life, but I damned sure wasn't going to have my ass nailed to a wall.

While I was outside the bar congratulating myself like some kind of dragon slayer, the bar had filled up some. When I returned, I rolled past tables of ones and twos. Every stool at the bar was occupied.

I took my place opposite Roger. He had changed into his Cardinals cap, pulled so low I thought at first he might be asleep. A man in bib overalls and a faded flannel shirt left his friend at a center table and walked over to stand between Roger and me.

"Hey, Jack. Nobody told me the circus was in town," he bellowed. His sidekick Jack laughed on cue. The overalls guy, who looked like he had swallowed a basketball, slapped me hard on the shoulder. "Fall off the trapeze?" he asked. He turned to Roger and pulled off his cap. "What happened to you, son? You must be the circus fire-eater."

Jack guffawed until he got the hiccups. Overalls shouted to his friend, "Take that mess outside. When you gonna learn to laugh like a human and not a monkey?"

Overalls jumped from one foot to the other, emitting sounds more reminiscent of a rusty pump handle than a primate.

"Leave the kids alone, Wally," said Eugene from behind the bar.

"Kids? They don't look like kids to me. Are you kids? How old? Twenty-one, twenty-five? Huh?"

Roger snatched his Cardinals hat from Overall's grease-covered hands. As he looked it over for stains, he said, "That as high as you can count, Wally?"

"Eugene, a couple of beers for my sassy friends."

"Leave them be," said Eugene.

"Oh, butt out. This is what drinking establishments are all about," said Wally. He placed a booted foot on the nearest wheel of my chair and rocked it back and forth. Easy at first, then in jolts. "A man meets a couple of strangers and after a few drinks, they leave friends. Right, boys?"

The tension was as thick as the cobwebs on the windowsills. Eugene laid down his towel and took slow, side steps toward the end of the bar. I grasped the wheel on the opposite side of my chair and pushed it forward as hard as I could. Wally's foot slid off the other wheel. He lost his balance and stumbled backward, landing on the table behind him, sitting in a puddle of spilled beer.

"Roger, help Wally up," I said.

The old guy kicked his legs and waved his arms like a big turtle stuck on his back. Roger stood up. He handed his cap to me. Jack gasped when he saw Roger's scarred head: the red, tight skin and small, uneven rectangles of thicker white skin, melded together. Roger leaned over Wally, still beached on the table. The old guy stared at Roger, his smart mouth ajar.

"Know how that happened to him?" I asked. No answer. "He did it himself. Set his own hair on fire. He loves fire more than anything."

Roger grinned into Wally's face and said, "I never seen a man's beard on fire." He sounded more like Bela Lugosi than a hillbilly, but the effect was as intended.

By now, Eugene stood in front of the bar. The men at the table where Wally had landed moved toward the wall. Jack opened the front door and stepped back inside. He had forced his face into a scowl to free him from laughing and annoying Wally again.

Eugene stepped forward and offered Wally a hand to pull himself up from the table. Roger backed away. Eugene looked down at me. "No charge for the pop. Maybe you ought to head home now."

I followed Roger toward the back door. As we passed through the storage room, Roger noticed the pelt on the wall. He turned and looked at me, his whole face a question.

Roger shivered. "Do you think it's her?" he asked. He reached his hand up toward the pelt.

"Don't," I said. "If it is her, let her rest in peace."

Roger nodded. He dropped his hand and picked up the ski poles. When we were outside, I said, "What are you going to do with those things? There won't be snow around here for months."

"I have an idea," Roger said.

37

GORDY

Roger drove his cousin's Buick to the end of the gravel driveway, where it intersected with Tanglewood Road. After sitting there listening to the tailpipe rattle for a minute or two, I looked at his silhouette in the dark and asked, "So, what's your idea?"

"Want to go for a little drive?"

"Sure. Where to?"

Roger looked straight ahead and grinned. "It's not so much where, it's how," he said.

He turned right instead of left toward the County Highway. He drove nearly to the end of the pavement, past the last house on the long, dark strip of road that seemed to narrow toward a point in the distance. A long black spear we were about to ride into the night, the future, the unknown.

Roger made a U-turn and stopped the car. He shifted into first gear and turned off the engine. "Sit tight," he said.

He exited the car and re-entered in the back seat. He sat on that half of a Packard seat and leaned over the back of the driver's seat. "Scoot over, behind the wheel," he said.

Confused but confident in my friend's plan, whatever it might be, I scooted my butt toward the left and dragged my legs. I eased myself behind the steering wheel and dropped my legs in front of the pedals. In the rear-view mirror, I watched as Roger lifted his arms, lowered them, then lifted only the left while pushing down on the right. Damned if I could figure out what he was up to.

Next, Roger grabbed the two ski poles and hoisted them—one in each hand—over the back of the seat. He set the end of one pole on the accelerator. The tip of the pole in his left hand touched the clutch. He pushed the clutch toward the floor to disengage the gears. "Change from first to second while I've got the clutch in," he ordered. "Pull the gear lever straight down."

"I know the gears. Uncle Phil taught me a long time ago. He used to let me shift his pickup when I was nine years old," I said. My voice sounded weak. Was this even possible?

We practiced several times, moving up and down through the gears so Roger could figure out how slowly to release the clutch without killing the engine. Positioning the knob at the end of the pole on the top of the clutch pedal provided the best leverage if he held his left elbow high enough to create as near a right angle between pole and pedal as the seat back would allow. Pure geometry or choreography? Either way, it worked.

"Can you move your left leg more to the left?" Roger asked.

I tried, but my leg still blocked Roger's view of the pedals. I switched on the interior light. "Better?"

"Some," Roger said. "The accelerator is still in the shadows. Can you cross one leg over the other?"

I tried lifting my right leg over the left, but that blocked the view of the ski pole controlling the clutch.

"Try tying your ankles together," Roger suggested.

"With what?"

Roger turned and looked around the floor where there was no back seat.

"Forget it," I said. "If the ankles are tied together, the knees flop apart."

Roger refused to give up. "Let's practice some more. I'll have to rely on the feel of the poles if I can't see the pedals."

This might have been the point where older, smarter, but lesser men might have shrugged and admitted at least temporary defeat. With the windows rolled down, we could hear bats squeal in the air above us. Were they laughing at the weak, wingless humans?

"Okay," Roger said behind me. "Start the engine, wheel man."

Roger's left ski pole mashed the clutch. I turned the key and the engine fired perfectly. I turned on the headlights. Take that, bats; behold the power of the human mind.

I studied the road ahead, or the few feet visible in the headlights. I noted a pothole on the right and the position of the ditches on both sides of the shining asphalt.

"Ready to do this?" Roger asked.

"Easy for you. If we crash, you can run away on two good legs. I'll be stuck in twisted metal until I starve to death," I said.

"Oh, I think someone would find you. It's the critters you have to worry about. You'd be like dinner on a spit to them."

"Shut up and let's drive," I said.

The steering wheel was so close to me. It felt intrusive. I thought about the Three Stooges movies where the steering wheel comes off in Curly's hands as he's streaking down a road. What happened to the Stooges? Oh yeah, they crashed.

"Pop the clutch," I said.

Taking off from a stop in first gear was a little jerky. Roger managed not to kill the engine. First to second was a breeze. The accelerator was easy to control with the right ski pole. Of course, Roger was a right-hander. Baseball builds powerful shoulders.

In third gear, I steered straight down the middle of the road. *This is how Buck Rogers feels in a rocket lifting off for the farthest star*, I thought. All my chains dropped away. I was pure motion. Sublime freedom. Everything was possible now. I was whole. I was normal. I was driving.

Apparently, this road was not on the top of the county's list for maintenance. Probably the only people who ever drove on it were drunks who made a right instead of a left turn trying to get home from the Bears Den. We rolled over a wide crack in the pavement, and my right leg flopped over, forcing the ski pole down hard on the accelerator. The car surged forward. At first, I was afraid to let go of the steering wheel even with one hand to pull my leg back. Roger pulled up on the right pole as I reached down to retrieve my errant leg. I knocked the pole out of his hand, and it dropped onto the passenger seat.

"Shit," Roger cried. The right pole was meant to operate the brake as well as the accelerator. "Grab the pole and hit the brake!"

The pole had now rolled onto the floor of the vehicle. As I stretched to reach for the pole, I lost my balance for a moment. I tried to pull myself back up with my left hand braced on the steering wheel. This action, naturally, pulled the steering wheel to the left and the car along with it. "Shit!" I cried.

Roger dropped the left ski pole and grabbed the steering wheel. This freed me to retrieve the right pole and push myself upright by shoving the pole into the floor. Grasping the pole with both hands, I pulled myself up with my buttock muscles and, like a whaler in *Moby Dick*, I harpooned the brake pedal. The car spun into the ditch and sputtered to a classic death. Call me Ishmael.

"Jesus, man!" Roger said. He slumped into the back seat and toppled toward the right door of our beached craft.

"We didn't hit anything," I said.

We were both quiet for a few minutes, each committing his perspective of the ride to memory.

"We flew, didn't we?" I said.

"Into a ditch."

"How fast do you think we were going? Top speed?"

"I wasn't exactly checking the speedometer."

"I bet 35 maybe 40," I said.

"In third gear? This tub couldn't hit 40 brand new," said Roger. He opened the back door and fell out onto the ground.

The laughter started in little snorts. Soon both of us were doubled over, heaving blasts of laughter into the night. I hung my head and arms out of the open window. Roger rolled in the ditch. Our laughter carried up to the treetops and chased the bats away. We saw a raccoon stick his nose into the unexpected light in his ditch and waddle away, starting a new crescendo of laughter. Our mirth contained notes of both relief and fear.

Roger walked around the car. "Nothing is broken, but we are definitely stuck. High-centered on the edge of the pavement."

"Any tires blown?" I asked.

"Doesn't look like it."

"Call my Uncle Phil. He has a chain. He'll pull us out, no questions asked," I said.

"I can't hike back to the bar and use the phone," Roger said.

"You're right. Wally would come out here and give us shit and drive away without helping," I agreed.

"No doubt. Well, there's bound to be a house somewhere. If not, I'll run to the highway and flag someone down."

The unspoken question hung between us.

"I'll be fine here until you get back," I said.

"Want me to take your chair out of the trunk?"

"You mean it didn't fly out? No, I'll be okay in the car." I scooted over to the passenger seat. "Next time, I'll tie my legs together."

The laughter bubbled to the surface again but did not take hold of us. Roger trotted away and soon disappeared into the darkness. I closed my eyes and remembered the feeling of flight at 40 miles per hour again and again.

38

PHIL

"Boys, boys, what have you gone and done?" I shouted after pulling his truck in front of the Buick. After surveying the position of the car, he declared, "No real damage done. Of course, on an old beater like this, what's one more dent, eh boys? We'll hook up the chain and be out of here quicker than a two-dollar fuck . . . Sorry boys."

As Phil worked to attach the chain, he noticed the ski poles lying in the ditch. "What in the world?" he said.

"They look like poles skiers use," said Roger.

"I'll be damned."

"Left over from the Ice Age."

"Eugene at the Bear's Den skis some. Hunts rabbits and such in the wintertime. Maybe they are his."

Uncle Phil pulled a chain from the back of his truck. He attached one end to the hitch and the other end to the axle of the Buick. He drove forward slowly until the chain pulled taut. It took several tries, going forward and then back, to set all four tires of the car onto pavement. Roger ran to disconnect the chain and return it to the bed of the truck.

Uncle Phil examined both axles and the wheels with a long flashlight. He told Roger to get in the car and drive forward a few feet. He wanted to see how it rolled. Satisfied that the car was muddied but sound, he walked over to the passenger window.

"What say we go on down to the Bear Den and have a beer? Soda pop for you boys. My treat."

"I think we better get home," I said. "It's late for a school night."

"I thought school was out for the summer?" Uncle Phil said.

"It is," Roger said. "Some parents keep strict bedtimes even in summer. Like mine."

The answer satisfied Uncle Phil and we were on our way to town.

39
GORDY

The living room in the Pardee house was cluttered. A pillow and rumpled blanket lay tossed on the sofa, used the night before by an overnight guest. Used glasses and plates sat on the coffee table. In the side yard, Mrs. Pardee's laundry was hanging on a line, drying in the breeze, still cool in the late July morning. A white blouse billowed like a lace sail. A 1946 Hudson Business Coupe with very low mileage was parked on the street in front of the house. It belonged to a doctor who preferred to ride a bus.

The phone rang.

Doc: Mrs. Pardee? This is Dr. Alger Dreesen. Is Gordon McCann at your home by any chance?

Me: Hi, Doc.

Doc: I'm calling to ask if you have heard from Jean today.

Me: Why? Is she all right?

Doc: I haven't heard from her, so I can't be sure. Her foster mother says she left without telling anyone in the house.

Me: You must be worried. I'm sure she is okay. Jean's smart, and she's tough.

Doc: I am aware of her intelligence and resourcefulness. This is very serious. She stole a car.

Me: Are you sure? Maybe she borrowed it. Did she leave a note?

Doc: As a matter of fact, she did. Let me read it to you: "Please don't look for me. I am fine. I will return your car as soon as I can."

Me: I didn't know you had a car. Don't you always ride the bus?

Doc: If there is a problem with Jean's foster family, I can help her. I haven't reported my car missing to the police. Yet. If she does contact you, please have her call me right away. Collect.

Me: Like I said, Jean did not call me this week or last week. I'm sure of that.

Doc: Please also tell her that her foster mother is holding off calling the police. The court appointed me as Jean's legal guardian. If the court decides I'm doing a bad job, she could be assigned to someone else. Someone who doesn't know her or care about her. Are you getting this, Gordon?

Me: Loud and clear, but I don't know how I can help because Jean did not call me.

Doc: One last thing: when you do hear from Jean, tell her she can keep the damned car. Just let me help her one more time.

Jean walked into the living room and began folding the blanket she had slept under the night before. I glared at Roger. He shrugged.

Doc: Are you still there, Gordy?

Me: Hold on, Doc. Here's Jean.

I held the receiver out to Jean. She shook her head until her copper curls were jumping. Finally, she took the receiver and spoke softly.

Jean: Hello, Doc. I'm sorry.

Doc: Why, Jean?

Jean: They all know about me. All the kids in the house know about my dad. I don't know how they found out. Maybe Mrs. Scott told them, or they overheard her talking to someone. Who knows?

Doc: Are they teasing you or bullying you?

Jean: No, the kids are cool with me. They have their own stories, some worse than my own. My dad never made me sleep in a cage and eat dog food. But, it's just a matter of time before everyone in south St. Louis knows about me.

Doc: I can fix this. I will talk to Mrs. Scott and remind her about confidentiality.

Jean: It doesn't matter. If the kids in the house know, the kids at school will know, sooner or later. You think the old man won't find me? He'll be out of prison before I graduate from high school.

Doc: I can and will protect you.

Jean: Let me stay here. Roger's mom is cool. Talk to her. Just a few weeks. Just until school starts. Please.

Doc: I'll have to check with a lawyer. I don't want to do anything to jeopardize my guardianship. Ask Mrs. Pardee to call me. Collect.

Jean: Thank you.

Doc: We'll talk soon. Have fun with your friends.

Jean: Gordy and Roger are good guys.

Doc: Agreed, but behave yourself. Tell Gordon he is a terrible liar.

40

GORDY

Jean really seemed to like Julie. I'm glad for my sister. They had their girl talk and sewed doll clothes together. Jean said Julie was jealous of all the attention I got after the accident. She also said Julie felt bad that she couldn't help me more, and she expressed it by tormenting me. That part sounded backwards to me, but Jean sounded very sure of her analysis. I wasn't about to disagree with anyone as beautiful as Jean.

Little sister Julie was drowning in resentment, but who could blame the kid? Her once unpopular brother was now a hero, a survivor, right? Every kid wanted to be my friend, right? Not exactly. More than once at the baseball field, a boy I didn't know pushed my chair to maximum acceleration and then pulled their feet off the ground, hanging from the chair handles with no control over the chair until he dropped his feet onto the ground and trotted to a stop. That's how teenage boys treat a hero? Girls expected me to hold their purses or sweaters while they stood at the dugout fence and flirted.

For the Perryville 4th of July parade, the high school band

teacher asked me to be honorary drum major. I was to wear a band uniform and lead the whole band down the street while pumping a sawed-off drum major baton up and down, up and down.

"When the band stops to play a song, you can roll your chair in circles or figure eights beside them," Mr. Mason said.

"Sorry, sir. My wheelchair is for indoor use only. My outdoor model is on order, but it won't arrive before the parade."

Mr. Mason paused before saying, "That's a shame. I hope it gets here before the Homecoming parade."

Julie loved tormenting me, more so after the accident than before. One Sunday, she invited a friend to come home with her after church. When we finished lunch, I heard the two girls talking on the front porch.

"Your brother is a dreamboat," the friend crooned.

"He pees in his pants, you know," Julie said.

41

PHIL

By mid-July, Henry making it to work on time was hit or miss. He slept at my place when he was too drunk to go home, which was often. Henry had a million excuses for his irresponsible behavior. His car was unreliable, but he couldn't afford to fix it. So, I changed all the fluids for him, greased what needed greasing, adjusted the belts, and replaced perfectly good spark plugs. I also cleaned a grocery bag full of empty whiskey bottles from the trunk of his car. I guess Henry didn't want Ida or the trashman to find them.

My place was no palace by any means. Just a farmhouse built by my granddaddy. My old man added electricity and indoor plumbing. The bathroom was built into the old laundry room behind the kitchen. I was used to the low water pressure and the rattling pipes. But, Henry complained every time he used the toilet or the sink. "The water in the sink runs so slowly that it takes half an hour just to shave. No wonder I'm late for work."

"I shave in the kitchen sink," I said. "The water pressure is better. It's hotter, too."

"Well, ain't you the prissy one?" he said.

Henry bitched about my cooking nonstop. I like to eat regular meals. By that, I mean eggs, bacon, and grits for breakfast, bacon and baloney sandwiches for lunch, and a thick pork chop or steak for dinner. The same menu every day. "It makes my grocery shopping easier. I never forget something because I always buy the same things," I explained. In the summer, I had a big garden for vegetables.

Henry followed me from one room to another, turning off lights I had just turned on. I told him I wanted the lights on. I spent too many nights in the pitch dark during the war, sleeping in one kind of field or another. "I fought for the right to light up my house the way I please."

I loved Ida and the kids dearly. I gladly took a turn nursing Henry through his alcoholic hell to ease their lives. But, when Henry started whining, "Woe is me, I crippled my own boy," once too often, I decked him and pushed his ass out the front door.

"You act like you're the one that got shot. Like you can't walk," I shouted. "Gordy's just a kid. He probably had dreams about playing baseball, climbing a mountain, fly fishing in the Ozarks, dancing with a woman. But, he can't, and he never will. I don't hear him crying and moaning. He's not pickling his liver every night and stumbling through his days. Goddammit, Sarge. I don't mean any disrespect. You're still my best friend. It's just that sometimes I can't stand the sight of you."

My helpful criticism was not taken as I intended. Henry pulled himself upright with the aid of my porch rails. He took a swing at my head and missed by a mile. He lurched across the yard to the gate and stood there trying to remember how to open it.

"Do you want me to drive you home?" I asked.

"No, no, no, thank you. I will sleep in my Fleet-muster. I am fine, fine. Where is my car? Never mind, I can find it."

"I'll wake you up for work tomorrow," I said. "6:30."

That was way before my peepers were ready to see the light of day. But, Henry stank to high heaven. I would have to stop by his house and get clean clothes for him.

At 6:30 am sharp, I brought Henry a fried egg sandwich and two Bayer aspirins. I offered to drive him to work, but he refused. As he backed down my long driveway, he hit an old sycamore tree. He drove to the shirt factory dragging a taillight.

Mid-afternoon, Ida called me at Earl's place. I told her he was okay, and I sent him off to work with nourishment.

"His boss's secretary called this morning. She put his boss on the line, who told me how sorry he was, but he had to let Henry go. He had no choice considering his recent behavior. He left it at, 'Please let him know I sympathize with what has happened, and if he can clean himself up, there's a place for him at the factory.'"

My heart hit the floor. "I saw him early this morning, but not since," I said. "I'll find him."

"Don't bother," Ida said.

"It ain't no bother."

"No, I mean, he's here. I see him moving around in the new house. I'm going to lock the doors. I don't want him in the house with the kids right now."

"Call me if you need me, Ida. Day or night."

42

GORDY

The last days of July were hot. On the twentieth, a Tuesday, the temperature was 104° at 4:00 in the afternoon. Luckily, our old house was comfortable enough with all the tall trees Grandpa planted around it. Sitting on the big front porch or near an open window with an electric fan running was my idea of "made in the shade." Mom said it was too hot to cook dinner, so she fried chicken or baked pork chops in the morning, and we ate everything warmed up in the evening. A big treat was homemade ice cream in the late dusk on July nights. I got teased into turning the hand crank because of my great upper body strength, but I really didn't mind.

Pop slept in the ruins of our never-to-be-completed new house. After losing his job and missing a couple of payments on the construction loan, the bank refused to give him any more draws for material or to hire workers. He puttered around some, hammering pieces of trim here and there. He slept there when he finally made it home from wherever he went to trade tools for moonshine. He couldn't afford civilized liquor anymore, so he hung out with old guys in barns and sheds and drank whatever he could afford. He thought he slipped home silently, but he usually managed to kick something over or set a dog barking as he passed a neighbor's house.

Mom carried on as best she could. Her sisters shared the vegetables they grew in their gardens. Once, Uncle Konnie went to the power and light office and paid our family's bill anonymously. Of course, we knew it was him. Mom cried to Aunt Eileen on the phone. She was angry that Uncle Konnie's paying our bill meant that everyone in Perryville knew or would soon know our financial condition.

"Someone from the power and light will mention it to someone else, and 'goodbye secret.'"

On the night of the twentieth, the new house must have been stifling hot. There was no canopy of trees to protect it from the sun. The walls had been framed but not insulated. Pop slept on batts of insulation on a sleeping bag. Cellulose insulation was made from ground-up paper and cardboard. It was treated with a flame retardant, but I doubt the manufacturers counted on the bonehead mistake of a drunk man smoking on a mattress of the stuff.

Because no one had air-conditioned houses then, they'd soak a piece of cloth in cool water and drape it over an electric fan. The damp cloth lowered the temperature of the air blowing from the fan. It works very well unless you are drunk. That's what the fire chief said happened to Pop.

He slept in the new house, in a little corner bed he made from planks and painters' tarps. The place stunk to high heaven. The water pipes had been installed. He had access to water, but there were no sinks or toilets. He took off around mid-morning and walked toward town to buy more booze. When he was gone, Mom would stash food and jugs of water for him. Probably what cash she had, too.

The fire chief told us that Pop must have mistaken a tin can of Turpoline™ paint thinner for water. When the fumes filled the air of Pop's bedroom and he lit his last cigarette before passing out for the night, he literally set the air on fire. The fire flashed up and burned away the fumes, but sparks from the fire fell onto the insulation, igniting Pop's bed and his clothes as well.

I woke up to Pop screaming. I got up and into my chair as quickly as I could. At first, I did not smell the smoke or was too startled to recognize the smell. The front door was open to let in a breeze. I pushed my way through the screen door and rolled down the ramp and into the yard.

Pop had managed to drag himself out of the room and onto the grass. That was the only good luck of the whole night. He rolled around in the dewy grass and put out the fire in his hair and clothes. He lay there unconscious while the house just behind him was engulfed in hissing flames. A dark gray smoke blew over him. I realized that when the house fell, as it would surely do and soon, burning lumber could fall on top of my father. No one deserves that kind of death.

I wheeled myself next to Pop so I could try to pick him up. I reached over the chair arm and grabbed the back of his shirt. The fabric shredded in my hand. I could not see him very well on the ground beside me. Smoke covered us both in seconds. I wanted to get Pop's body across my lap so I could roll the chair away from the house. I couldn't tell if he was unconscious, but he wasn't helping me at all. I had to be careful pulling him up so that his weight would not cause my chair to tip. If that happened, it would be a double funeral for sure.

I shouted, "Raise your arms, Pop. Raise them toward my chair."

I heard screaming from inside the old house. Mom was awake.

Pop raised his arms a few inches, but it was enough. I was able to pull his upper body onto my lap, but his legs were still dragging on the ground.

I heard a siren in the distance. Mom—or a neighbor—had called the fire department. I felt relief for only a moment and continued pulling more of Pop's body onto my chair. When I thought I could try to roll the chair, I reached down for the right wheel rim, clutching Pop with my left arm. Even if the chair moved sideways, it would be away from the flames. I did not expect the metal hand rim to be searing hot.

Mom came running up to where I was stranded with Pop.

"I can't touch the rims. Too hot," I shouted.

Mom scooted behind my chair. She pulled the sleeves of her robe over her hands to grasp the handles and pushed with all her strength. She managed to move the chair only a few inches before a fireman ran up behind her and took over. He pushed the chair out of the way just as the house collapsed on itself. Embers flew into the air. They scorched the grass where I had just been sitting. Once we were out of harm's way, I shoved Pop onto the ground. He landed with a thud but did not wake up. The fireman heaved Pop over his shoulder and carried him to the fire truck and started giving him oxygen. Mom checked me high and low for injuries, but I was fine. I noticed the ends of the sleeves on her robe were singed.

When the fire department finished soaking what little was left of the house, the captain found me and congratulated me on saving Pop's life. He asked if he could call the *Perryville Republic Monitor* and have them send a reporter to interview me. Just as I opened my mouth to say, "Sure," Mom threw a huge fit, swearing at the captain.

"Mind your Goddamn business. We don't need the whole city knowing about this. Are you taking my husband to jail?"

"No, ma'am. We are taking him to the hospital. There will be an investigation as to how the fire started, and the police will determine if charges are appropriate."

"I'm so sorry," Mom said. Now the tears started to flow. "I've never used such language in my life."

"It's okay, ma'am. You would be surprised what people say and do when they are afraid. We'll keep pouring water on the fire most of the night to make sure it doesn't flare up again."

I thanked the captain. Julie had been watching from the old house. She threw open the screen door and ran toward Mom. Together, we helped Mom walk back to the house. Julie found some burn ointment and put it on Mom's hands. Mom insisted on sitting in the kitchen in case anybody needed anything.

Once Pop was driven away, I was aware that my right palm was burned. I rolled myself to the bottom of the porch ramp, leaned over the left armrest, and yanked up some damp grass. It felt good on my burned palm. Later, Julie put ointment on my right hand, too.

I remembered Roger saying that his house reeked of smoke for weeks after the fire that burned him. He said the smell kept his mother on high alert. She would sit up straight and sniff the air, then run from room to room touching doors, feeling for hot spots.

I hardly noticed the smoke of the campfires, barbecues, and cigarettes I had been exposed to all my life. The smell of hickory smoke from a grill was one of my favorites. After the fireworks on my birthday, the sulfur hung in the air all night. When we drove past an old house, Pop said the smoke from the wood stove in the house reminded him of Grandpa McCann. "He believed until his dying day that fire in a cast iron stove, if properly built, was safer than any gas furnace."

"It's a concrete slab, again," I said of the once new house.

"I'm sorry Dad burned your house," Julie whispered.

"It was never *my* house, you know."

"Yeah. I just called it 'Gordy's house' to tease you. To make you laugh and not feel so sad about what happened to you."

"Not just me, kiddo. Something happened to all of us that day."

"I think I was a little jealous," she said. She pulled her legs up under her and snuggled closer to me.

"I just don't understand why you would be jealous. Look at me. My life—or what I thought would be my life—is over. What I have to look forward to is never, ever walking again. I won't grow anymore. Did you consider that? No sports. My shot at the Olympics is never going to happen. Half the buildings in town I can't even get into. Too many stairs or no elevator. Want to hear the worst part?"

"No."

"The worst part is I can't look at someone eye-to-eye. Not unless they sit down. That means if I want to talk to someone out in public, I get to talk to their belly button, or worse, their crotch. How would you like to face a future like that?"

"I'd hate it," Julie said. She was seconds away from laughing.

"It's not funny," I said, pretending to be angry.

"Talking to a crotch is VERY funny."

I extended my hand slowly. She leaned her face toward me, thinking I meant to wipe a tear or touch her cheek to comfort her. At the last second, I squeezed her nose, pulled my hand away, and showed her my thumb between two fingers. "Ha! Got your nose."

Julie batted my hand away. "Stop it."

"How about some ice cream?"

"Oh no," she said.

"What? Don't worry. I told Mom I would look after you. I'm in charge, and I say we deserve ice cream."

Julie pointed to the dining room. "Your chair is a mess."

I looked behind me. The back tires were misshapen. "The tires must have melted a little," I said.

"The back of the seat came loose from the frame in a couple of places. See?" she said.

"Dammit," I said.

"No ice cream for a cusser," she said.

Julie jumped off the sofa and ran into the kitchen. I heard the freezer door open and the silverware rattle as she opened the drawer. For the first time, I noticed my arms were sore, and I was very tired. How could I get my chair fixed? Pop was no help now. Uncle Phil and Uncle Konnie both worked. Maybe Roger could drive me to a wheelchair mechanic somewhere. But how was I supposed to get around the house without the chair? For the first time in a long while, I felt handicapped.

Julie returned to the living room carrying two bowls of Neapolitan ice cream. Mom always bought that kind because she said it was "three in one." Julie handed me the bowl that was entirely strawberry and dug into the chocolate mountain she had carved out of the carton for herself. I pictured the little wall of vanilla left in the carton. Mom always dipped Neapolitan ice cream vertically so each person had a bowl with all three flavors.

"Thanks, kiddo," I said.

Julie swallowed her ice cream before she answered. "I only teased you because I didn't want to cry all the time. I hate Dad for shooting you. Now, I hate him more for burning down your house."

"He did not do either intentionally," I said.

"You forgive him?" she asked.

"I don't know for sure that Pop shot me, so there's nothing to forgive. Burning the house was his fault, definitely."

"Mom will never forgive him for that," Julie said. She scooped up a big bite of chocolate ice cream and filled her mouth. She turned to me on the sofa, opened her mouth, and growled. A little stream of ice cream rolled down her chin. She clamped her mouth closed. For some reason, I found it very funny.

43

I rushed over to the McCann place just after dawn the morning after the fire. A buddy in the fire department called and told me about the fire and about Henry. What a mess I found. The house we worked so hard to build was a pile of black, smoldering spiky wood. All the insulation was burned. How anyone got out of that alive was beyond me.

Ida was in the house drinking iced tea. She had been at the hospital with Henry until all hours. When she finally did get home, she wasn't able to sleep. The ice in her tea had melted long before I showed up. I took the glass from her to refill it and noticed the palm of her hand was red and swollen. "How did that happen?" I asked.

"Gordy's hand is worse."

"Is he at the hospital?"

"He refused to go in the ambulance with his dad. Would you take him to Emergency and have them take a look at his palm?"

Ida filled me in on the details. I wanted to cry, but I could not swallow my anger at Henry. I still could not hate him, but I sure wanted him to feel some of the anguish he was causing his family. Now, Henry had something else to feel guilty about.

"We've got no insurance on the house," Ida said. She sat down at the kitchen table. "Because the construction loan was delinquent, the insurance company will refuse to pay for the fire damage. This whole place stinks of smoke. How do I get rid of that?"

"I'll set up some heavy-duty fans to blow it out, but you might end up having to repaint at least the living room. Don't worry. Konnie and me will take care of it."

"There's no money to buy paint." Ida sobbed into the collar of her robe.

"You let old Phil worry about those details. You take care of yourself and your chicks."

We sat silently for a while. I heard Gordy stirring in the dining room. Ida looked at me suddenly and said, "Oh my God. His chair. What if it was damaged?"

"Let me take a look at it. Get dressed and put some things in a bag. I'll take you to a motel," I said.

"I've already called Eileen. We'll go to her place for now, and Julie wants to stay with Viv. That will be better for her. Those twin boys get on her nerves, I know. Mine too, sometimes. Will you go see about Gordy? If his chair is broken, you'll have to carry him ..."

"I know. Go on up now and don't rush. I'll check on our boy and his chair. Then I'll make us some breakfast," I said.

Ida stood up from the table and carried her glass to the sink. As she turned to walk by me, she leaned down and kissed my forehead. "I take back all the bad things I ever said about you, Phil Toomey."

"What bad things?" I pretended to be hurt. Ida smiled at

me like she never had before. A little gratitude turns me into a workhorse. I went to see if Gordy was awake before I started anything as terrifying as cooking breakfast.

At the Perryville Hospital, they checked Henry out and treated his burns, which were not as serious as they could have been. He was so drunk it was a wonder he got out of the house on his own. Wonder, too, that he didn't run back in to get whatever hooch he had hidden in there. When Henry stumbles, lots of people take a fall. I'm thinking of Ida and their kids.

I admit I kinda liked playing the rowdy uncle, but even I knew when to set the bottle down. Once I asked Henry how much booze it would take to make him stop and sober up. He shoved me and told me to leave him alone. Sure, I wanted to just walk away and have nothing more to do with the sarge. But, dammit, if I wasn't around to take a blow once in a while, how much more damage might Henry have done to himself and his family?

I drove Ida, Gordy, and Julie to the hospital. Jim and Viv met us there to take charge of Julie. The doctor treated Gordy's hand and loaned him a wheelchair until we could get his cleaned up. I went for coffee and returned to find Ida and Jim talking to Sheriff Guillaume in the visitor's room. Ida kept shaking her head "no," and Jim kept nodding "yes." I decided they needed a tiebreaker. I had no wish to butt in, even less to talk to Jim, but duty called.

I nodded to the sheriff. We had spoken before. Jim took a step back and folded his arms across his chest. He reminded me of how kids act when they want to avoid cooties. He had been around children so long he picked up their habits. What a jackass. "Tell me what you need, Ida," I said.

She sighed deeply and shrugged. "I don't know myself. The

hospital wants to release him and the sheriff wants to arrest him."

Jim said, "He has to go somewhere, at least for the night."

"What are the charges?" I asked Sheriff Guillaume.

"The evidence so far doesn't support arson. I don't think Henry set the fire intentionally. If not, there won't be charges for insurance fraud."

Jim unfolded his arms and stepped forward. He was taking the lead now. "Fraud is a pretty weak charge. How much jail time would Henry get? If he's found guilty, of course."

The sheriff put his notebook and pen into his shirt pocket. "As far as the county is concerned, Mr. McCann had no intent to harm anyone except maybe himself." He turned to Ida and asked her, "Has he talked about harming himself?"

"Certainly not."

Jim leaned forward toward the sheriff. I guess he thought he'd been deputized. "You really should talk to the people he worked with," Jim said. "He was just fired from a management position."

Sheriff Guillaume wrote something in a little notebook. "I'll put him in a cell for tonight. Maybe by tomorrow after-noon I can talk to him. In the meantime, Mrs. McCann, can you find the insurance policy on the new house? A construction loan always requires insurance."

"I will call the bank tomorrow and find out," she said.

Jim put his hand on Ida's shoulder. "I would be happy to make that call for you. There's nothing more you can do for Henry tonight. I'll drive you home. Do you have anything in the house to take to help you sleep? Probably not. Why put temp-tation in Henry's way?" he crooned. I thought I might vomit. I could always blame it on smoke inhalation.

I don't know why I was so pissed off when Jim butted in and took charge. He always acted like his shit didn't stink because he went to college. I shoved my revulsion aside and turned to Ida. "Call me if you need anything. Any time. Promise?"

"Of course, Phil. You really are the truest friend to us all," Ida said. She started crying and nearly fell onto my chest. I held her best I could.

"You know what?" Jim said. "Phil can drive you and Gordy home. I'll get Vivie and Julie out of this place. Sheriff, if you need me, I'm in the phone book."

I had to focus on the family. Jim's sudden interest was just to get information to share in the teacher's lounge.

44

PHIL

Henry ended up staying in jail two nights. I drove Ida to pick him up and took them to see a lawyer. Eileen made an appointment with the attorney who represented Modern Homes. His name was Ken Bassett, and his second-floor office was across the street from the county courthouse. I offered to wait in the car, but Ida wanted me to come in with them. "I don't trust myself to remember everything the lawyer says. You can remind me." What could I say?

"I am not a criminal attorney, you understand, Mr. McCann. I've worked with your brother-in-law Konnie for a number of years, and he asked me to have a general discussion with you."

"I appreciate you taking the time, sir," said Henry.

Mr. Bassett sat behind the most beautiful walnut desk with more little carvings and gee-gaws than I ever saw. Across from the desk was an old church pew stacked with files and law books. Mr. Bassett explained that it had been his family's pew from a couple of generations back. I suspect he liked it not for sentimental reasons but because it was so uncomfortable that clients didn't linger asking a lot of questions. I seated myself on a church pew for the first time since—well, a long time.

"I contacted the County Attorney to see if he was preparing charges. He told me that he intended to bring charges under Section 569.065, which is negligent burning. I doubt Henry would be convicted since he was not competent when the fire started."

"I'll just plead guilty. What kind of a sentence does that carry?" Henry asked. His legs were shaking almost as much as his voice.

"Well, it's a Class C misdemeanor, so no more than a fine, I would say. Since no one was injured and there were no damages to a third party, the County Attorney said he was inclined not to press charges if you agree to go to a rehabilitation facility for your alcohol use."

"Yes, I want to do that," Henry said. The relief poured off him like a waterfall.

"Excellent. Contact him for the particulars. He mentioned the Salvation Army facility in St. Louis. They have an excellent reputation, from what I have heard. Don't worry, you won't have to bang a drum on a street corner." Mr. Bassett chuckled. His joke appealed to an audience of one. But it was good news, and he did not charge Ida for the advice.

As we walked to my car, I told Henry he could stay with me until things were set up with the Salvation Army place. Ida had made it clear she did not want Henry to come home until he had dried out. "Try to get some rest. There is no liquor in the house at all, so don't go nosing around and upset my immaculate housekeeping." Poor guy, he was so wiped out he didn't even smile.

The next morning, I dropped Henry off at the gas station. Earl said he would keep an eye on him. "Drunk or sober, he can pump gas and wash windshields," Earl said. Henry seemed eager to be helpful. I headed back to Ida's place. My top priority was to see what could be done about Gordy's chair.

Konnie's employees had already removed the fire debris. The wind was calm and that was a blessing. The charred dust didn't blow around much. The men had covered the huge black stain on the concrete with a tarp.

In the house, Ida was serving Raisin Bran cereal to Gordy and his girlfriend Jean. She offered me a bowl, but I turned it down. "Where is he?" Ida asked.

"He's helping Earl this morning at the station," I said.

"Your grandfather is a saint," she said, handing me coffee.

I leaned close to Ida and whispered, "If Henry starts acting like a fool—crying or shaking so bad he spills gasoline on a customer—I gave Earl permission to knock him out with a wrench."

I gave Gordy's wheelchair the once-over. It was in better shape than I expected. Steel won't melt in a puny house fire. Though the rubber tires were shot. "I can probably replace them with bicycle tires," I said.

"See if the tires on my old bike will fit," Gordy said.

Jean beamed and joked, "You thought you wouldn't ever ride that bike again." She wasn't being mean at all. It was a pretty good joke. Even Ida smiled.

"I'm glad I did not sell it to Calvin," Gordy said.

"Okay," I said. "Let's see what else we need to do."

I measured the wheels and wiped the chair down good. The caster wheels in front were fine. Some of the stitching on the back of the chair had pulled out. That was easy enough to repair. Ida had pulled a pillowcase over the back of the seat. The bicycle tires fit the rims, and we all watched Gordy roll around the dining room. Julie begged for a ride on his lap to test the tires.

It was time to rescue Earl, but I wanted to talk privately to Ida. She and Jean were outside hanging laundry on the line.

"Are you okay for groceries?" I asked Ida.

"Yes, for now. Viv and Eileen brought us some chicken and hamburger. I've got plenty of canned vegetables. Jean's going to help me make biscuits from scratch later."

Jean shook out a dress and pinned it onto the clothesline. Ida and I took a few steps back. We spoke in low voices.

"I know Henry feels guilty for what happened to Gordy. Even if it wasn't his bullet, he feels he should have protected his son. Since the accident, he feels so helpless, worthless. So, he punished himself," I said.

"By drinking and getting fired? By burning down Gordy's house?"

Jean turned toward us. "My father was an alcoholic, and worse. He could only see things from his point of view. That's how Dr. Dreesen explained it to me," said Jean.

When Ida turned to look at Jean, I saw little streams of tears on her cheeks.

"I had no idea, dear," Ida said.

"Dr. Dreesen says he needs to be in a hospital while he withdraws from alcohol. It's a pretty bad time. My dad went through it more than once."

Ida dropped the wet shirt she was holding. "You talked to Dr. Dreesen about this?"

"He's my guardian. I tell him what is on my mind. Especially when it concerns my boyfriend and his family."

I watched Ida's face muscles soften. Her jaw relaxed and her shoulders dropped. She reached out for Jean and they held each other. Who could watch those two strong gals and keep crying? Not me.

"I'll tell Henry," I said.

Ida turned to me without dropping her embrace of Jean. "No, I'll tell him. After I talk to Dr. Dreesen. I think everything should be arranged before we tell Henry, so he can't refuse or make excuses."

"You and Gordy should tell him together," Jean said.

Ida picked up the wet shirt she had dropped and handed it to me. "Jean will show you what to do with this. I have to make a long-distance call to St. Louis."

She turned her back and marched toward the house. Jean handed me a clothes pin. "Know how to work these?" she asked.

Two women telling me what to do. The world was coming back to order. I felt for the first time in months that things were going to turn out just fine.

45

GORDY

Pop was in a hospital in St. Louis for nearly a month for him to dry out. Only Mom saw him during that time. She did not tell us anything except that Pop missed us and wanted to see us as soon as he was able. One night after Konnie brought Mom back from visiting Pop, she knocked on my bedroom door.

"Gordy, are you awake?" She spoke softly in case I was asleep.

"Come in, Mom."

Mom sat on my bed. "Would you like to visit your dad?" she asked.

"Won't I just make him more depressed?"

"You don't make him depressed. Never think that. Jean was right. He has been punishing himself for what happened to you. For months he's tried to numb his mind with alcohol, to stop thinking about what kind of life you are going to have. I told him that no one knows what the future holds. Imagining the worst, even to defend against it, doesn't help. While we're fighting one problem, another one is sneaking up where we least expect it."

"I don't blame Pop," I said.

"I know you don't. I don't blame him, either. It's just that I felt so overwhelmed when he started to fall apart. I felt like the responsibility for everything was falling on me. I guess I resented it and that's why I didn't see ..."

"Stop right there. What you told Pop goes for you, too."

We sat in our own thoughts for a while. After a few minutes, I realized Mom was rubbing my legs. I smiled at her. "I like that you are touching me. I can't feel it the same way I used to, but I do know you are doing it. I can see your arm move and I know it means you love me."

We both started blubbering, and then Mom stood up. "Can I ask a favor?"

"Sure, anything."

"Can I try the chair? I've wanted to try it for a long time, but it seemed a silly thing for a grown woman to do."

I pulled myself up in bed. "This I gotta see," I said.

Mom sat down in the chair. Only her toes touched the footrests. She grasped the handrims and pulled back. The chair rolled back just a couple of inches. "Oh, my. It's much easier than I thought," she said.

"Okay, now push forward just a little," I said.

She pushed forward and moved closer to my bed. Her knees were touching my mattress. I didn't say anythingbut let her figure out her next step. Sure enough, she rolled back, pulling more with her right hand than her left. This made her turn so she was parallel to my bed. The bedroom door was still open, but she had to maneuver the chair around the end of my bed to straighten up the chair enough to go through the door. My hands clenched and released several times, but I did not say anything. Mom steered around the bed and out the door like a drag racer on Sunday.

"Come back," I called. "I'll need that when school starts."

From inside my room, I heard the chair rolling around the dining room table. Mom was laughing out loud. She rolled into the living room and squealed when the wheels caught going from hardwood to carpet. I nearly wiped out there a few times myself.

"What's going on down there?" Julie called from the top of the stairs. She must have seen Mom roll back into the dining room because she squealed, "I want to ride, too!"

I was stuck in the bedroom. "I want to see," I called.

Mom walked into my bedroom pushing the chair. "Come on, then. We'll get you a ringside seat."

I scrambled into my chair and went into the dining room. Julie had dragged a chair next to me so I could transfer and watch the action. "My turn, my turn!"

Julie, being smaller than Mom, had a little trouble getting the leverage she needed on the handrims. Her arms just stuck straight out over the armrests. Mom trotted into the living room and returned with the St. Louis phone book. "Sit on this and see if it helps," she said.

After Julie was seated on the phone book and tied into the chair in case the book slid, there was no stopping her. She circled the dining room table, then did a 360 at the living room door and came back and circled the table again.

I called the action: "Driver in the purple robe has taken the lead. She's unstoppable on the turns around the table. Oh, now she's being flagged by the pink robe to come in for a pit stop. Now, they've changed drivers. Pink robe is off without losing precious seconds."

46

GORDY

Jean had settled in nicely with the family. She sewed with Julie and Aunt Viv, who worked for Modern Homes now. Jean helped sew curtains for the model homes and something called "table runners." The three of them had a weekly Friday night sewing party. One Friday, Aunt Viv drove Julie home and stayed for coffee with Mom. I sat on the porch with Jean. It was a really hot night, and even with two box fans strategically placed and blowing at full force in the dining room, the dark porch was cooler. Porch lights attract bugs, and electricity to run fans costs money. Also, no one could see us if we kissed.

"Roger's mom thinks it's a good idea for you to visit. Might speed your dad's recovery if he knew you were cheering for him," Jean said.

Jean had suggested I visit Pop a couple of times. I put her off by saying Uncle Phil was too busy with his garden and work at the station to drive us. Roger had baseball practice every day, and I doubt Uncle Jim would give Aunt Viv permission to drive that far.

I was so afraid of losing Jean, but I'm sure she knew I was avoiding the subject. This time, in the darkness where I could not see Jean's disappointed face, I finally told her the truth.

"I don't want to go there and say, 'Everything's fine, Pop. Take your time getting back to your responsibilities.'"

"That's pretty lame, but it's honest I guess," Jean said coldly. This was exactly what I feared would happen.

"I'm sorry. I'll go if you want me to," I said. That really ticked her off.

"If you don't want to, then I don't want you to, either. Listen to us. We sound like idiots."

I reached for Jean's hand in the dark. There was enough light from inside the house to see it, but it was kind of fun. I said, "I know you give Pop more slack than anyone because of what your old man was like."

"No comparison," Jean said softly.

"I have told Pop several times that I don't blame him for what happened to me. I talked to the doc about it. I told him I didn't mind another operation to get the bullet out of me so we could settle it once and for all."

"What did he say?" Jean asked.

"He said, and I quote: 'No can do.' Actually, it was more like 'unnecessary surgical risk.' Doc said scar tissue had grown around the bullet by now. It's nice and cozy wherever it is," I said. My attempt at humor was wasted.

"Doc is the expert."

"I'll ask Roger to take me. He's got to put that baseball down sometime. You'll come, too?" I asked.

Suddenly, Jean turned to face me and kissed my cheek. I felt like I was in an episode of *I Love Lucy*.

"I know he will drive us. He hits a baseball like a killer, but he's a softie. You should see how sweet he is to his mother."

I rolled back and forth. My gimp version of kicking the dirt and saying, "Gee whiz." A road trip would be very nice. "I wrote Pop a letter after the fire," I said.

"What did you say?"

"I didn't send it. Want to read it?"

"Only if you want me to."

I spun around and rolled toward my bedroom. Jean did not follow me. She had never been in my dining room *boudoir*. Jean said my mom would not approve of her being in my bedroom if it were upstairs, and she didn't want to take advantage of the weird situation. I returned with an envelope. It was not addressed and had no stamp.

Dear Pop,

I don't have any more ways to tell you that I don't blame you for the accident. I wish you could believe me. I guess we both got hurt in ways that will change our lives forever. I'm not going to try to cheer you up. I used to hate it when the nurses said to think about all my blessings. I thought they could never understand how I felt. It made me mad that they would try. The first time I transferred from my hospital bed to the wheelchair, Clayton clapped and danced around the room. Weird, I know. But I got the message. I celebrated my tiny little achievements and they started to add up to real progress.

What I'm saying, Pop, is I would do anything to make you feel better. But, it wouldn't mean anything. The only things that really help are what you do for yourself. We'll celebrate every good day. You'll see how fast they add up into good weeks and months and, even, a good life.

Love,

Gordy

I watched Jean read the letter twice. The first time her eyes were full of tears. After the second read, she sighed and said, "This is beautiful, Gordy. It's wise."

"I used to think the accident happened only to me. Not true. It affected lots of other things, other people."

With that insight, I earned another kiss.

Roger pulled into the driveway with Jean on Sunday. He cut a dashing figure wearing a Branch Rickey-stylebatter's helmet. Made of hard plastic, it had a tab on one side covering the ear. Roger was a right-hander, but he wore the helmet of a lefty. The flap covered his right ear, hiding his burn scars. Jean said it made Roger look more handsome than the bear hunter hat he usually wore. Roger blushed as red as the cardinal on the helmet.

We found the address where Pop lived, his sober living house, deep in Dutchtown, South St. Louis. It was one of those big box houses with small windows and a wide porch, made from red clay bricks. Roger said the row of thick, squatty houses on Michigan Avenue looked like a defensive line in a football game. Pop's house was in the middle of the block. Roger called it the inside linebacker position.

"I thought you were a baseball player," Jean said.

"A guy can know two sports," Roger answered.

"No curtains on the windows and no flowers in the yard. It's a cinch no women live here," Jean said.

"It's a halfway house for men," I explained. "They live together as roommates and share the cooking and cleaning chores. They have to keep a job and pay rent."

I set up my chair by the open car door. As I swung into it, Roger walked around from the driver's side. Jean wanted to wait in the car until she was sure a lady was permitted in the house. Roger asked why it was called a halfway house. "Because it's halfway between detox and the outside world. You need to take that plastic bowl off your head."

Roger looked down at me and said, "We better look for a back door. You're not getting the chariot up those four stairs to the porch."

He took off around one side of the house. That left me on the sidewalk, staring at the concrete steps. Before Roger returned, one of Pop's housemates opened the front door. He looked down at me from the summit of the stairs and smiled. "You must be Henry's boy."

"That's right. I'm Gordy."

"I'm Robert. Henry told us you were coming. We are prepared!"

Robert was older than Pop by several years. His dark hair was thin and starting to turn grey. He had a friendly smile, missing only one tooth.

Robert reached behind the porch bannister and pulled out a long piece of lumber. He slid it down over the steps and secured one end under the lip of the porch floorboards. Then, he pulled out a second plank and put it into position over the stairs.

"Now, line up your chair at your end of the planks so I can make sure I have the spacing right," he said.

The planks extended several feet beyond the stairs and onto the sidewalk. The ends of both boards had been planed down some, making it easier for me to mount the ramp. The parallel planks were wide enough to support my bicycle tires with inches to spare on either side. Roger moved behind me in case I needed help to get up the incline. Jean had exited the car and stood on the sidewalk. She covered her mouth and held her breath. She acted like it was a rope bridge over the Grand Canyon I was climbing.

The extra length of the boards made the slope easy to

ascend. My Charles Atlas upper body strength was tested, but I rolled steadily forward. When I reached the end of the porch floor, I pushed my weight back, lifted the caster wheels, and quickly leaned forward as I gave the wheels a big push to get me over the lip of the porch. Jean applauded. Roger ran around the side of the house to see my big finish.

Robert held the front door open for me, and I rolled easily into the living room. "It's just that easy," I said.

Roger and Jean walked up the stairs in the space between the boards of my ramp. They found seats inside, and we basked in the glow of our can-do resourcefulness. Robert excused himself and went into the kitchen. "Lemonade for everyone," he crowed over his shoulder.

Pop and I met from opposite sides of the living room. I was just inside the front door. Pop stood in the kitchen doorway. I couldn't exactly run into Pop's arms, although I sure wanted to. He had lost weight. His face was thinner, and it sort of ran into his neck. He looked humbled but not defeated. We looked at each other and nodded in approval of what we saw.

After a great dinner of grilled pork chops, fried apples, and sliced tomatoes from the house garden, Roger and Jean volunteered to help with cleanup. Pop and I sat together on the porch. At 6:30, the temperature was still 90°. Pop commented on the breeze from the southwest and the low humidity (38%) because all Missouri men include at least a mention of the weather in every conversation. It might be required by law. I did notice that the porch, with its three-foot brick wall around the outside, was very comfortable, but said nothing.

"Cool ramp, Pop," I finally said.

"One of my roommates works at a lumber yard. We all

chipped in to pay for it. We are going to make a picnic table for the backyard next."

"So, it's okay here?" I asked.

"Saved my life."

"Where do you work?"

"I do maintenance and some groundskeeping at Cleveland High School. It's an easy walking distance."

"Different from the shirt factory, I'll bet," I said.

"It's better right now. I work with one other guy. He's all right. I'm learning a lot of new skills," he said.

Pop leaned forward in his chair. He rubbed his hands together in his lap like he just could not get them clean. He lifted one foot toward the top of the porch wall. He loved to sit with his feet on a box or footrest. He stopped his foot about halfway up the wall and set it back down on the floor. He cleared his throat to fill the silence. If I could not prop up my feet, neither would he. Though it really made no difference to me. "Be comfortable," I told him.

"How's Julie?" Pop asked.

"Good. I think she might even be a little less annoying. That's Jean's influence, I'm sure."

"Jean's a peach," Pop said. He smiled for the first time since we arrived. "How is the rest of the family?"

"Uncle Konnie says to let him know when he can come visit. Aunt Eileen talks to Mom at least five times a day on the phone," I said.

"What about Viv and Jim?" Pop asked.

"Aunt Viv is working. No kidding. Uncle Konnie hired her as a designer for his show houses."

"Jim must be livid," Pop chuckled. "He treats her like she's twelve years old. I think that's so she won't challenge him."

We talked about school starting soon and what classes I would take. I told Pop that Jean was living with Roger's family and that Dr. Dreesen had arranged it. We would all three be going to Perryville High School after Labor Day.

"Does the doc know where I am?" Pop asked.

"Jean asked him to get you into the hospital, so he knows. I haven't talked to anyone about you. It's nobody's business where you are."

"This place is good for me," he said.

"Uncle Konnie and Uncle Phil cleaned up the mess from the fire," I said.

"Tell Konnie I will pay him as soon as I can."

"He doesn't want to be paid," I said.

"I have to pay my rent and my share of the groceries here. That's the rule of sober houses. I don't make much, but I will pay him back every cent. Please tell him."

I guess I had exhausted my good behavior for the day. I did not want to talk to Pop anymore. Try as I might, I just could not feel sympathetic about a situation he'd brought on himself.

The sun was low in the sky, but it was a long time yet until dark. Roger and Jean walked around the neighborhood. I thought they were getting restless to go home.

"I want you to know that your mother doesn't deserve any of this, not from me," he said. His hands returned to his lap, and his head hung forward.

I said, "Mom can forgive. She taught me that. You did, too. You both forgave Uncle Phil every time he made a mess of something or tried some boneheaded scheme."

"Phil is unique. He has a good heart and always means well."

After another uncomfortable silence, Pop said, "Part of the sober house program is group therapy."

"Oh yeah?"

"I hated it the first few times. I was determined not to whine and moan in front of other losers. One night, someone said, 'You know, a .300 batting average is considered pretty great. But it also means failing to hit the ball seven out of ten times. If a baseball coach can forgive seven out of ten mistakes, why can't we?'"

"I forgive you, Pop," I said.

"And you saved my life, pulling me out of that fire."

Pop stood up and faced me. He knelt down and hugged me so tight my lungs started screaming for air. That's love.

Pop was back in his chair, and we had both wiped away tears when Robert came onto the porch. Roger and Jean joined us, too.

"I'd like to get home before too late," Roger said.

"An athlete needs his rest," Henry said. "What was your batting average this summer?"

Roger grinned. "A solid .335," he said.

"Nice going," Pop said. "I told you this kid will be drafted by the Cardinals the minute he graduates."

We sat a few more minutes, and I excused myself to use the bathroom.

"Need any help?" Pop asked.

"Nope." I swung my chair in a perfect 180 turn and opened the screen door for myself.

When I returned, a couple of the other roommates were on the porch. One of them said, "Pretty fancy tires you have on that chair."

"They're bicycle tires," I said.

"No kidding?"

Everyone took a closer look at my tires. Jean said, "He wore the old ones down with all his sharp turns and trick spins."

"Uncle Phil fixed me up with these. They came off my old bike. Remember, Pop?"

"Sure. Phil is a mechanical wonder," he said.

Roger tapped his batter helmet. "He found this for me."

"Very chic," Jean said as she tapped her knuckles on the helmet.

I rolled down the ramp unaided. Pop and the guys followed us to the car. After they watched me execute a perfect transfer to the passenger seat, Pop folded my chair and put it in the trunk. Roger waited through another round of goodbyes and best wishes, and we were homeward bound. We traveled in silence until we reached 61-South, when Roger started singing a terrible Elvis impression of "That's All Right."

47

PHIL

I was elbow-deep in a customer's transmission when Earl yelled, "Call for you, Phil. Long distance. Hurry before they hang up."

I wiped my hands on a rag as I walked across the garage and into the office. Just a few long strides.

"Earl's Petroleum, Phil speaking."

"It's Henry."

"Hey, Sarge. You're a sight for sore eyes—that is, glad to hear your voice."

"This is long distance," he said, clipping his words to save time. "Listen fast. What do you know about Ida selling the lot for the new house?"

"Not much," I said as quick as I could.

"Got a letter here from a lawyer with a contract for a sale. Wants me to sign."

"Ida needs the money," I said. Talking fast was sure blunt.

"You talked to her about this?"

Henry's throat was really tight, I could tell. He always tried to keep his anger out of his voice, but I could always tell when he was trying to control his voice.

"Konnie found the buyer," I said. Maybe knowing Konnie was involved would help reassure him. "You know what I think happened? The lawyer jumped ahead and sent you the papers on his own. I'll bet Ida doesn't even know he sent papers to you."

"Maybe," said Henry. "Conversation's over."

"I'll talk fast. Two words: friendly fire. Could have been me; could have been you who fired the shot. It happened. Are you going to spend the rest of Gordy's childhood thinking about yourself or how to help him?"

"Mind your own business."

"Call Ida. She's a strong girl. Don't wait until she doesn't need you anymore. Call me. Collect."

I stopped by to see Ida the next Sunday afternoon. I picked up a few groceries on the way. Roger and Jean were there, so we made ice cream. After supper, Ida and I sat outside under the trees. Jean and Julie were sewing in the dining room. It was a secret project they did not want anyone to see until it was finished. Gordy and Roger sat on the front porch playing poker for pecans. I had brought a bag of nuts from the tree on my place. I intended for the boys to crack them for Ida, not gamble with them.

It was still muggy, but I noticed the leaves on the maples were not as deep green as they were just a few days ago. "Fall's coming," I said.

"I love all these trees. When they reach their high color, and the afternoon sun moves across the yellows and dark reds, it takes my breath away. I call it God's bouquet."

After a few quiet minutes, Ida said, "Henry signed the sale papers. He called to say he sent them to the lawyer. The money will sure help."

"I'm glad for you," I said.

"He wants to come home. He asked my permission. It scares me a little. How do I know if he is ready? I can't take much more upset this year."

"He's worked hard to get himself well," I said.

We cracked some more of the pecans and visited until dusk.

48

GORDY

On the Friday before Labor Day weekend, Uncle Phil drove Mom to pick up Pop at the sober house. Julie wanted to go along to see Pop's apartment. "If Daddy isn't going to use it, maybe I could live there," she said. Mom laughed out loud. Her laugh sounded good after so long a dry spell. Mom was a lot like Aunt Eileen, but thankfully less strict. Their voices were set at a lower pitch. Not like a man's voice, just a very determined woman's way of talking. People said they could hardly tell Mom and Aunt Eileen apart on the phone. Aunt Viv had a more quiet, breathy voice. I used to think she talked like a little kid because Uncle Jim treated her like one. Mom said when she was a kid, Aunt Viv realized she could not talk over her sisters, so she went the other way.

Jean and I were alone in what we continued to call the old house. Roger drove her over but could not stay because he needed to help his father with some yard work. That's what Roger said. More, that's what Roger and I practiced he would say. School started on September 6th, the Tuesday after Labor

Day. Who could say when Jean and I might have the house to ourselves again before we turned middle-aged?

We began the afternoon sitting on the living room sofa, listening to the hits on WIL A.M. radio from St. Louis. Jean wore pedal pusher pants, so we could sit nice and close to each other.

"Are you nervous about school starting?" Jean asked.

"No. I'll get to use the freight elevator. The janitor uses it to move furniture and trash, I guess. They bring food up to the cafeteria on the elevator, too. It's right by the back door."

"How will you get to school?"

"Not sure yet. Probably not on the bus. Uncle Jim has taken charge of working that out."

"What if you could roll your chair down the middle of the street to school? It's not that far," said Jean. She was getting excited about the idea. "Of course, the city would have to close down the streets for you."

"A police escort seems fair," I added.

Jean's favorite song came on the radio: Ricky Nelson's "Be Bop Baby." She jumped up and started singing in front of the sofa. She swung her delicious hips right and left. When she danced, the curls on her forehead bounced. When the song finished, she fell back onto the sofa, blushing.

"Ms. Jean Beaumont, Perryville High School's 1955 Homecoming Queen," I announced. Jean laughed and blushed again. We both caught our breath when Sam Cooke started singing "You Send Me." Jean snuggled up close to me, and I put my arm around her shoulders.

"I'm so glad you're here in Perryville," I said. "Sophomore year is looking pretty good now."

I leaned toward Jean. She scooched closer to me, and I

turned my torso as much as I could. She met me more than halfway, and we kissed, albeit a bit awkwardly. We needed to be facing each other, not parallel. Mathematicians like to say, "Two parallel lines will eventually come together, but it takes effort." I pulled my right leg up on the sofa and then the left. Now I was facing Jean's left side with my legs straight out in front of me, which made us perpendicular. Jean turned to face me, but my legs were in the way. Jean had to turn to her left, pull her legs under her butt, and lean precipitously close to losing her balance to embrace me. "Not very romantic, is it? Two dead legs in the way," I said. Undeterred, she leaned into me. We kissed for at least twenty seconds.

Jean pulled back and said, "I have an idea."

She removed the magazines and hard candy bowl from the coffee table. The white doily under the bowl she folded carefully and placed on the arm of Mom's side chair. Then Jean pushed the coffee table toward the sofa until they touched. The height of the seat of the sofa exactly matched the top of the coffee table. I am certain that Mom made sure this was so.

I twisted my upper body so my legs could rest on the coffee table. Jean helped me move them to the coffee table one by one. I was embarrassed to have her touch my limp legs, but she did not flinch. Now I was sitting at a thirty-degree angle to Jean. Better, but we were not finished. I scooted so that my right butt cheek was at the very edge of the sofa. This created a little pocket of space between me and the back of the sofa. Jean fit perfectly into the little nest.

Jean and I necked until I felt the unmistakable urgency of an erection. Nothing new, but could I sustain it long enough to see the thing through? I had no idea. Nor did I want to try and fail, not on my first outing, and not with dear, beautiful Jean.

I stroked her silky neck and unfastened the top button of her blouse. No resistance, so I went on to the second button. The skin below Jean's neck was a little moist. We were very close together, at 98.6 degrees each. So far, I was holding up my end. I reached for the third button, and Jean pulled away. She folded her legs against her chest and snuggled against me. Her face and neck were not out of reach. For my part, I remained at the ready in case she changed her mind in the next minute or less.

Jean said softly, "Did you ever wonder why Dr. Dreesen is my guardian?"

"No," I said. I prayed my voice would not break.

"When I was younger, my father hurt me. Dr. Dreesen worked sometimes at the Veterans Hospital. My dad lost a leg in the war. The doc treated him there."

"What happened?" I asked. I felt her begin to tremble, so I locked my arms around her waist and let her answer when she was ready.

"I can't tell you now. Maybe someday. Anyway, the doc arranged for my father to have the rest of his treatment in Kansas City. My mother went with him. She blamed me for breaking up our family and hurting my dad. She said I should not have tattled to Dr. Dreesen. But I didn't. He saw for himself. Anyway, they just left me alone in the house. I was about six years old. I called the hospital and told them I was alone. The doc contacted people who could help me. He asked the court to make him a *guardian ad litem*. It's Latin for someone who takes care of a kid until the court can get the family back together.

"He found a family for me to stay with, and he checked on me often. As I grew up, we became close. He signed my report cards, took me shopping for school clothes, and helped me get a library card. I was about nine when my father started calling me. Because he had not terminated his parental rights, he could still visit anytime, and no one could stop him. One day I got a letter from my dad. Well, not a letter, but he sent me dirty pictures through the mail. The doc lost his mind when he saw them. I was so scared my dad would come back to St. Louis and make me go to Kansas City with him. There was nothing to stop him.

"The doc went to Kansas City on the train. He never told me what happened there, but he came back with the papers signed by my parents, giving me up permanently. Then he became my legal guardian until I turned twenty-one. I never lived with him, though."

As Jean told me her incredible story, her voice became stronger. She stopped shaking. When a tear fell off my chin onto her neck, she said, "Don't cry, Gordy. I am okay now. I love the Pardees. I have a big brother there. Well, two counting Julie."

"You are a great big sis for Julie. She had a hard time after my injury. I guess I got most of the attention around here for a while."

Jean pulled herself up and faced me. She kissed me on each cheek, my forehead, and then so sweetly on my impatient lips.

"I just realized that the doc introduced you to me when I was at St. Anthony's. You thought I was a wet rag back then."

"No, I thought you were cute. Kind of."

Jean pulled herself out of my arms and climbed over my legs. "We better put things back before your folks get home," she said. While she moved the coffee table, I transferred to my chair. When she finished, Jean turned around and announced, "I have another idea."

"Oh, yeah?"

"You mentioned Homecoming."

"So I did."

Jean turned up the radio and pushed my chair into the dining room. "If we are going to the Homecoming Dance, don't you think we should practice?"

I was not sure what she had in mind, but I was getting an idea of my own.

Then we heard the radio announcer: *Now, boys and girls, here's a real rockin' tune by the hippest hipsters around. You know them. You love them. Bill Haley and the Comets with "Mambo Rock."*

"Stand in front of the chair," I said. "Face me. Stand on the footplates."

"On your feet?"

"You won't hurt me."

"I'll at least take my shoes off," she said.

Jean climbed onto my shoes. I held her hands. She wobbled a little at first. "Relax," I said. "Put your hands on my shoulders."

It looked awkward, but Jean played along. I began to rock the chair very gently. Jean yelped when the chair started moving.

"My butt will stick out." Jean laughed, nearly losing her balance.

"Soften your knees. See, that's better. Now, hold on. I'm going to turn wider, left then right."

I pushed one wheel while holding the other still, then switched. We were both feeling the music in our bodies. I added a back-and-forward motion. Jean moved her hips to balance my moves.

"Ready for a big finish?" I asked, nearly breathless.

"Burn rubber."

"We're going around the world. Keep your knees soft."

I executed a smooth 360 turn. Jean shifted her body weight with me. Ta-da!

We heard the rumble of Uncle Phil's truck in the driveway.

"Quick, go to the table," Jean said.

Uncle Phil called from the driveway, "We're home." So subtle, giving Jean and me warning to make ourselves presentable if necessary. He opened the kitchen door and ushered the family into the house.

We took our places at the dining room table. Jean jumped up and ran into the living room. She grabbed a *Life* magazine from the coffee table and raced back. She started reading aloud from an article: "What Science is Doing About the Perils of Radiation." I nodded with intense interest.

When everyone walked in through the kitchen, Jean was reading aloud: "In response, nuclear scientists from around the world will meet to discuss establishing an international agency to study the effects of radiation from an atomic blast on human beings." That's my girl. She picked the most unromantic article imaginable. My ardor cooled; saved for another time. In spite of everything, it was the best night of my life. I have always been glad I did not try to rush into something neither one of us was ready to try.

Jean ran up to Julie and hugged her tightly. "Julie! You came back to me. What happened? The apartment didn't suit you?"

"Nah. It's just a bunch of old men like Daddy. Kind of creepy all of them together like that."

"Julie!" Mom cautioned. She looked exhausted. When her eyes flashed like they did just then, Julie knew she was close to big trouble. We all were.

"They cooked a nice supper for us," Julie said. She pulled a lint-covered dinner roll from her skirt pocket. She must have been sitting on it the whole ride home because I only recognized it as some kind of bread from its sweet, yeasty fragrance.

Jean begged Uncle Phil for a ride home. I did not protest her leaving me alone to face the family. Mom set about checking on everyone's physical comfort. Did we prefer the front door open for the breeze or closed to block the view of the vacant lot across the yard? In the descending dusk, the raked dirt lot was barely visible. Mom closed the door.

"Anyone for a snack or drink?" she asked. Aware of the current tight budget, they all swore up and down they were too full from supper and not at all thirsty. She asked Pop directly, "Would you care for iced tea?"

He answered, "No, but thank you for asking."

We stood in a circle facing each other. No one moved or spoke. It was obviously too early for us to split up and go to our bedrooms or, in Mom's case, into the kitchen. "I have an idea, let's sit down together and watch television," Pop said. "Julie, would you mind checking the *T.V. Guide* for us?" I wondered if Pop had missed us all so much over the last few months that he wanted to immerse himself in our company, or if he needed us to confirm that he was welcome to stay.

Julie called from the living room. "*Wagon Train* just started." It was a good choice—stories of families searching for a new life. Members of a wagon train heading into the unknown West. Strong men and women facing unforeseen perils in the hope of a better future together. That was the show for us.

When the people in the wagon train reached their destination, it was time for the McCanns to face sleeping arrangements. Julie rushed up to her bedroom. Pop stretched in front of the sofa and said, "I'll stay here tonight. I don't want to disturb anyone if I get up in the night. I'm a little wound up from packing and the drive home."

Mom looked relieved. "Gordy's old bedroom upstairs is available if you prefer. I took the liberty of setting up the roll-away bed in case it might be needed."

When people are nervous about being together, they often resort to more formal ways of speaking. All those extra "pleases" and "thank-yous" are like little bricks we stack in front of ourselves to make a protective wall. Mom sounded like she was auditioning for a play by Shakespeare—"in case it might be needed." Believe me, I'm not criticizing her. Mom stepped up and managed the family and all its chaos since last April. It was a huge responsibility, and without Pop's weekly paycheck (or presence), she had her own pain from the accident to deal with and no privacy to deal with it. Now it was my turn.

"I have something to say. I've been thinking and working this out in my mind all summer."

"Of course, son," Pop said.

"Last April, you two both lost the son you thought you had. Gordy the Normal, with all his working parts, was suddenly gone. He's not coming back. I faced the loss of myself; who I thought I was and who I wanted to become. But here I was. Here I am. So how can I be gone if I still think and talk and learn and laugh?

"I challenged myself to become strong, to make the most of what I had left physically. I think I did okay, and I will keep getting better with your help. So, before we drown ourselves in loss, how about taking a look at what we have left? We still have our home, our brains, and our love for each other."

I credit Jean with showing her courage to speak about her deep pain. I like to think she would have been proud of me if she had heard my words. Jeez, I wished she were standing beside me right then.

I was not finished. "Pop, you can use my bedroom here on the first floor. I've been hankerin' to bunk in my own room. I even trained for it. Watch and be amazed."

I called out to Julie, "Hey, little sis, come see what old Gordy can do."

I rolled to the bottom of the stairs. I turned the chair so my back was to them. I set the brakes. Scooted my butt forward in the seat. I removed my belt from my pants. I pulled my knees toward my chest. I held my knees with my chin while I secured my legs with the belt around my thighs and my calves. I pressed my left hand onto the second stair behind me. I pressed my right hand down on the seat. I swung my butt out of the seat and onto the second step. I steadied myself on the stair. I grabbed the edge of the third stair with both hands behind me. I pushed my body up and sat on the third stair. (Thank you, Charles Atlas.) I repeated until I was sitting on the top stair.

I looked down at Mom and Dad. They were not hugging, but they were standing closer together. Julie let out a "Yippee" that woke the neighbor's dog.

"Dad, if you would be so kind as to bring my chair up the stairs. I'm rather fatigued and wish to sleep in my own bedroom."

Pop folded the chair and carried it up the stairs. Mom was right behind him. I transferred from the floor to my chair, facing backward, to thunderous applause.

"This is a one-night deal," I said to my parents. "Tomorrow night I want my first-floor room back. Why share a bathroom if I don't have to, right?"

And so, the McCann family members were once again in their places—for the most part. We were like the board game Julie got for her sixth birthday called "Sorry." The object was the same for all the players: to move their plastic pieces from the start position all around the board to the home position. You might get to slide several spaces forward if you were lucky enough to land on the right square. Or, you might be sent back to the start with a heartfelt "Sorry" from the player who sent you there. Always, we kept picking a card, whether it sent us forward or back, because the only way to get home was to keep playing the game.

Acknowledgments

I needed to visualize the daily challenges of life in a wheelchair. I wanted to portray as accurately as possible the ways Gordy used his chair most efficiently in his daily life on two wheels. Thanks to the following organizations and individuals who shared their life on wheels through Internet videos:

- National Center on Health, Physical Activity and Disability.
- https://NCHPAD.org - Videos including "How to … With Mary Allison"
- SCI Empowerment Project Wheelchair Video Series (Joshua Hancock)
- https://sci.washington.edu/empowerment/videos.asp
- Adapt to Perform https://adapttoperform.co.uk (videos)
- KanduGroup -- info@kandugroup.com

I am indebted to Shoshana Sumrall for editing a draft of *Wheel Man*. Also, thanks to Katie Vincent for the final edits. Her critique and suggestions helped me write my best book.

ABOUT THE AUTHOR

Marcia Calhoun Forecki is a native of Kansas City, Missouri. She earned a master's degree in Latin American Studies and attended the University of Nebraska MFA program.

Her first book, *Speak to Me*, is a memoir about discovering her son's deafness. Published by Gallaudet University Press, the book won a Book Award from the President's Committee on Employment of the Handicapped and was used in educator training courses for many years.

In 1997, Marcia was one of fifty finalists (out of several thousand entries) in The Chesterfield Film Company's Film Project.

Her novel *Blood of the White Bear*, a medical thriller co-written with Gerald Schnitzer—a New York producer of films, documentaries, commercials, and a writer/director active from the 1930s through the 1950s—was a Willa Award finalist in 2013. Sadly, Schnitzer passed away at the age of ninety-nine shortly after the novel's release.

Marcia's stories have appeared in print and online in *Bellevue Literary Review*, *The Copperfield Review*, *Writers Foundry*

Review, *Eclectica*, and in two anthologies. Her story "Consolation" was a finalist in the 2024 Women on Writing Contest, and "Ozark Son" was longlisted by *History Through Fiction* in 2024.

She served for more than a decade as a contributing editor to *Fine Lines* literary journal and is a member of the Board of Directors for Larksong Writers Place in Lincoln, Nebraska.

Follow her publications and events at www.mcforecki.com.